A DROP OF DREAM

BOOK ONE OF THE TALENTED SERIES

AMY HOPKINS

Cover by Valerie Chambers

This book is a Spellscribe Press Production

Amy Hopkins

50 Eudlo Road

Mooloolah Valley, Q, 4553.

Print ISBN: 978-0-6489761-0-3

*This book is dedicated to those who joined me on this journey,
but no longer walk beside me.*

*Dad, I miss you so much. You were never a reader, but you embraced
my love of words as hard as I gripped the words themselves. You
believed in me, you supported me, you let me make so many mistakes,
and you knew who I was before I ever did.*

*Lyss, I know I will forever be a better person for knowing you. We all
will. You were a beam of pure light in our lives, leading up forward in
the darkness even when distance and time separated us. You always
said we were the kind of friends who could pick up after years like
nothing had happened... but now I regret those missed years deeply.
Miss you.*

DO YOU HAVE THE WHOLE TALENTED SERIES YET?

A BOGGART'S JOURNEY*

A DROP OF DREAM

A DASH OF FIEND

A SPLASH OF TRUTH

A PROMISE DUE

A FESTIVE DAY*

WHEN MAGIC FADES

*denotes short stories in this series

Fancy free reads and exclusive content?

Make sure you're on my mailing list!

You can sign up for updates and offers at:

www.amyhopkinsauthor.com

www.facebook.com/thespellscribe

www.twitter.com/spellscribe

Chapter One

The damp pavement glittered under the first kiss of morning's light as I stepped outside. The air still held a touch of mist and I rubbed the goosebumps on my arms. Despite the chill, I smiled. The sight of early-morning London never lost its charm, even after years of living here.

"C'mon, Lenny," I called.

Lenny bounded over, his too-long legs and floppy ears making the effort look clumsy, if adorable. I scratched his head, then pushed it away as he sniffed my basket.

"It's just teas," I told him. "Keely said she needs some Soft-Sleep and three boxes of Awaken on top of her usual order."

He snorted appreciatively, then perked up as someone approached.

Well... some*ones*. Pax and Tox, two of my demigoblin customers, strolled towards us. The brothers looked like every other demigoblin in London, with their green, baggy skin and bulging eyes, but I could finally tell them apart – thanks to an unfortunate encounter with a cat, its milk, and the permanent scar that now graced Pax's left cheek.

"Mornin', Emma!" Pax called. His gruff voice made it hard to tell what sort of mood he was in, and his deeply wrinkled face didn't suggest much, either. Still, his pointed ears hung limp—I'd learned from experience that when a demigoblin's ears stood forwards, it was best to tread carefully.

"Morning, Pax." I waved with my free hand.

"You openin' soon?" Tox asked. "I need some Luck."

I narrowed my eyes. "What for? You know I won't sell anything that lets you cheat."

He grinned. "I'm meetin' a lady tonight. Don't want to trip on my face or have a swarm of angry 'oney-badgers pop up to ruin the night."

"Honey-badgers?" I shook my head, laughing. "I don't think you have to worry about that, Tox."

Pax joined in with a hearty chuckle of his own. "I told him, there's no chance of that happenin' twice in one month. Well..." He looked at his brother. "*Almost* no chance."

I lifted my basket. "I just have to run this over to Keely's. Come back in about half an hour?"

Pax and Tox both nodded and went on their way. Lenny and I set off, quickening our pace after the short delay. The tea shop had been getting busier of late—my trade with the Otherworlders had always been strong, but as the stigma of being part-Talented slowly wore away and people became more accepting, I'd gained an influx of curious mortals wanting to try the magical effects of my tea.

Just yesterday, a trio of young businessmen had come to sample my blends for Alertness and Calculations. They'd bought a single box to share but returned minutes before closing to buy every last leaf on my shelf.

By the time I rounded the last corner, my cheeks were flushed and the biting London air seemed a little warmer. A row of tenements stretched along the narrow street and I hurried toward number twenty-six – Keely's house.

I approached the worn red door, unable to stifle a sigh at the rubbish piled beside it. Empty bottles lined the front step and a pile of cigarette ash filled one of them. *Oh, Keely. You're never going to give up on him, are you?* Sensing my abrupt change in mood, Lenny gave my leg a comforting nudge.

Keely's father was a heavy drinker. They often fought about it, but she refused to move, insisting that if he didn't have someone looking after him, he wouldn't last the week.

I knocked on the door and waited. Beside me, Lenny whined.

"It's ok, boy." I gave him another head scratch. "It's just Keely's. You've been here before."

When no one answered, I tried again, thumping harder. If I didn't get back to my shop soon, I'd be late. When your customers include trolls and ogres, it's best not to piss them off.

I raised my hand to knock a third time and jumped when it cracked open.

"Whaddyawant?" Keely's father, Ernest, sported at least a week's worth of rough stubble and his eyes barely opened.

"I've got to drop these off to Keely," I said. "I told her I'd be around early this morning—is she up?"

"See fer yerself." He turned and stomped away, leaving me to push the door open.

Lenny pressed against my side and whined again.

"Wait here, boy. Stay." I stepped inside, nose wrinkling as strong fumes hit it. Rum, probably, and old beer.

I picked my way through the mess. I hadn't been inside the tiny flat before, and Ernest had already slumped back into a snoring heap on the tattered couch.

Taking a guess, I tapped lightly on the pink-painted door hung with feathers and sticks. When no one answered I cursed under my breath and checked my watch.

I've got fifteen minutes before those demigoblins start beating on my door. Stealing a glance at Ernest snoring away, I debated leaving the basket outside Keely's door. Ernest didn't know about Keely's attempts to sober him up, though, and I couldn't be sure of his reaction if he dug through the teas to find the addiction-enchanted box.

After knocking one more time, I slipped out my wand.

Keely and I weren't close. She knew I didn't approve of her curse-selling business and thought my own rules for selling 'took all the fun out of magic'. Still, we had a friendly professional relationship.

Hopefully, that relationship would survive the early morning intrusion. Waving my wand in the pattern that would trace my spell, I dismantled the simple charm that kept the door locked. I pushed it open.

This room smelled different. Sage and lavender, and a hint of vanilla permeated the warm air. Unlike the cluttered space outside, Keely's room was a more organised chaos. A corner desk stacked with boxes sat beside a worktable strewn with twigs, string and feathers. The closet was ajar, held open by a bundle of scarves dangled over the door, and the room glowed pink from the sunlight behind vibrant curtains pulled shut over a small window.

"Keely?" I stepped quietly over to the silent lump under the covers.

She didn't stir, so I carefully placed the basket on the bedside table. In trying to balance it amongst the clutter, I knocked a lamp. It teetered and before I could grab it, it fell to the ground.

The soft clink of broken glass sent my heart into my shoes.

"Dammit!" I whispered.

I couldn't leave now—there was nothing in the room to clean the glass up with, and I didn't want to go skulking around the house looking for a broom.

"Keely!" I called a bit louder and reached over to shake her.

Her skin was cold and stiff. My heart thumped a hard beat and I swallowed a sudden lump in my throat.

"Keely?" I asked again, the confidence stripped from my voice.

I pulled her shoulder and the body rolled towards me. Blank eyes stared at the ceiling and an inch-wide hole gaped under her collarbone.

It took me a moment to realise the high-pitched scream was mine.

CHAPTER TWO

Detective Charles Greyson jotted down another note, his face grim. "What about her dad?" he asked, again.

"I've already told you—I know he's got a bit of a drinking problem, but Keely never said anything to make me think he was violent." I absentmindedly reached out to stroke Lenny's head and he thumped his tail, happy for the attention. It eased the ache in my heart, just a little. My frustration, however, hadn't abated.

The detective had arrived with one other person. No forensics team, no back up. Though Greyson had at least poked around and asked what seemed like a million questions, his companion had simply peeked at the body and then elected to wait in the car – filling out paperwork, he claimed.

"And all that mess in the living room?" Greyson asked, pulling my attention back to his interrogation.

I shrugged, then wiped my nose. "It was a cluttered mess when I came in. When I screamed, Lenny came bolting in. He's... not very coordinated."

Lenny's ears perked up at the sound of his name, and he gave Detective Greyson a wide, panting smile.

Greyson narrowed his eyes at Lenny suspiciously. "There was no sign of a forced entry when you arrived?" It was a new question, but his tone suggested he knew the answer already.

"The door wasn't blasted to pieces or anything, no. I wouldn't know what else to look for. *Officer.*" I added the last as an afterthought, then bit my tongue when I realised the word had come out rather snidely. *Cool it, Emma. He's not the bad guy. Just... probably not a very helpful one.*

"Do you have a problem with the police force, ma'am?" Detective Greyson asked blandly.

Problem? Apart from the fact that not one of you give a damn about my dead friend? Nerves getting the better of me, I shook my head. There was no way I was going to risk getting myself arrested.

He sighed and put his pad away, then looked me over. "I'll get in touch with the relevant department."

Anger prickled at me, flaming my grief and fear into anger. "Of course you will," I muttered.

Greyson looked wounded. "Look, I'm just a regular copper. These kinds of things are out of my jurisdiction."

"Bullshit." I stood and turned away, but my emotions got the better of me. I turned back.

"You're just like the rest of them." I gestured out the door, where officer number two sat eating a sandwich. "Do you think I'm stupid? I read the papers, I know Keely's death is just another in a long string of them. But we're half-bloods. Nobodies. You'll kick this over to those useless twats at the O.C.U. and wipe your hands of a case that was too much effort to follow through."

I knew I was right. When Arthur, the first victim, was found there was an uproar. The idea of using magic to kill wasn't a new one, but this had happened outside of the cloistered Inner City, and that meant regular people might be at risk.

By the time the second and third deaths had rolled around, and the regular humans realised all the victims were half-blood... none of the unTalented were at risk. Suddenly, the front page story became an addendum at the back. The Otherworld Crime Unit, a bunch of washed-up rejects who weren't quite bad enough to be fired from their policing jobs, hadn't come up with a single lead.

The Talented, those high and mighty lords who lived behind the walls of the Inner City, wouldn't lower themselves enough to care about a dirty half-blood. Despite the fact we shared half our genes with them, the intermingling of pure magical blood with a common mortal was anathema to them.

"That's not fair," Greyson said. His dark eyes searched mine. "It's not that I don't care. I really can't—"

"Can't and won't are two very different words, Detective Greyson." I stood and gestured to Lenny. "If we're done?"

He hesitated for a moment, then nodded. "Someone will be in touch."

"I very much doubt that." His heavy gaze settled like a weight on my shoulders as I left, but I knew I was right.

No one cared about the half-bloods.

CHAPTER THREE

"Another attack?" Pax asked. "Thought they'd have caught him by now."

"You know how it is for us." I tied a neat string around Tox's parcels and slid them across the counter. "There's no one to turn to. Is there anything you can do?"

Tox grabbed his tea, his ears forward and alert. "We'll keep an eye out, make sure the Others report anything suspicious. Don't want our favourite tea-shop shuttin' down."

Pax's beady eyes shot open in alarm. "You're not gonna shut shop and run are ya? Your Speedin' tea is the only thing that keeps me faster than the Balrogs when I go huntin'"

"Not a chance Pax." I gestured at the shelves beside me. "This place means everything to me, I wouldn't leave it. I appreciate the help, though."

Pax grinned, showing his crooked teeth. "Don't mention it. You know you've earned your place here and you've always looked after us. We'll keep an eye out."

I knew he meant it—Otherworld creatures took things like honour and loyalty seriously... even if they didn't have the same respect for concepts like ownership or personal boundaries.

Tox handed over his chips, the currency of the Otherworld, and I busied myself getting their orders ready. I made a quick note of the sales in my ledger and waved goodbye.

Outside, tyres screeched as a car slammed on its brakes. I looked up to see a nine-foot-tall half-giant waving a sheepish apology to the car she'd nearly stepped in front of. Despite the vehicles having been around for over a century, the Otherworlders still struggled with the basics of road safety. Mavis waited for the car to pass, then headed into the shop.

"Mavis, I haven't seen you for weeks! Is everything... well?" I wasn't sure how else to phrase the delicate question.

Mavis, hunched over to fit her large frame into my tiny shop, blushed. "Yes, m'lady. I'm with child. Three, actually."

I flew around the counter to embrace her. Having brewed various teas for the local Giant clan for a while, I'd been surprised to get a request such as hers. Mavis, being a mixed-breed of two different clans, had been having trouble conceiving. A standard human fertility tea would have helped somewhat, but I'd tweaked the spell I'd used on it to account for the slight variance in giant anatomy. I hadn't been sure if it would work.

"Three? Is that typical?" I didn't think it was.

"No, m'lady. If all goes well and they survive, I'll be able to gift one to each of the major clans. I'll be looked upon quite favourably after that." Mavis perused the selection I had on display. "I do hope you have something for the tummy upset, though."

Despite my discomfort at the child raising customs of the giants, I was happy for her. She spoke little of her personal situation, but I'd gathered her place in the giant hierarchy was quite low because of her mixed birth. That was something I was painfully familiar with.

The day continued, all manner of creatures visiting my little tea shop, and not all were coming in to buy tea. The news that I'd had a brush with a serial killer had travelled fast.

London was a busy place, a central hub that acted as one of the major thoroughfares between the Otherworld and our world. They shared information freely and the topic of what the humans were up to was a frequent topic of conversation between them. Though this made for an interesting mix, we generally existed together in peace. Generally.

Trouble came a short while before lunch. I'd just waved over Jacoby, one of the few Talented lords who frequented my shop. Old and wheelchair-bound, probably due to some magical disease or curse, he seemed to have more empathy for half-bloods than most of his kind.

"Bye, Hent," I called, waving to the kobold on his way to the door. He ducked his head as he reached for the doorknob just as a small, flying piske flung the door open with a spell. It caught Hent in the face.

"Oh, gods," I whispered.

Hent grabbed the piske with lightning fast reflexes but was immediately blinded by a sparkling bomb to the face. He roared, letting go of the smaller creature, and stumbled around trying to swat him out of the air. Instead of the piske, he batted my light fixture.

"STOP!" I ducked behind the counter to avoid the kobold's grasping hand.

This did not bode well for my shop. The piske, determined to fulfil the orders given to him by his master, didn't leave. He zipped around, staying just out of Hent's reach as he lumbered around the tiny, enclosed space.

Hent swung an arm and I ducked to avoid being hit. He crashed into a shelf of boxed teas, and I screamed as it came crashing down, just missing my head.

"So help me, Hent, if you don't stop this *right now...*"

I raised my wand despite having no idea how to stop an enraged kobold, but paused when I saw Jacoby's already out, tracing a delicate pattern in the air. I waited, my own defences at the ready.

His spell took about a second and a half to trace. Both Otherworld creatures dropped to the ground. They were conscious but woozy, and neither could stand. Jacoby wheeled his chair over to them and looked down. "You both have about twelve seconds until you can walk—or fly." He looked at the piske. "At that time, it would be best if you both left, in a calm and orderly manner. My next spell may not be so gentle."

True to his word, the two were shortly up, and out of my shop. Jacoby turned discerning eyes my way.

"Thank you so much," I breathed. "I may have been able to stop them myself, but not before they caused more damage. I'm in your debt."

"Nonsense, my dear," he said. "A simple spell. Cast in my own interests, I might add, as I don't have my own order yet."

"The usual?"

"Please."

I packaged up the same tea he ordered every week—two boxes, both for pain. It made me sad that this kind man had been reduced to using simple charms to manage in his daily life.

Though I abhorred most of the full-blooded Talents for their elitist, bullying ways, Jacoby seemed different. He was always polite, and never looked down his nose at me. Most of the Lords from the Inner City thought themselves beneath shops like mine and sent servants like the piske to collect their goods.

As he left, Gibble came in. He growled at Jacoby. "Nasssty human."

"Gibble!" I snapped, alarmed. "Be nice to the customers."

Gibble could be off-putting—he was a boggart after all—but he was generally polite. Or at least, not outright rude. Gibble had been helping in the shop since I'd opened it, and this was the first time he'd had such a strong reaction to a customer who wasn't out to cause trouble.

The day progressed and my shop got busier, but I couldn't keep my mind off Keely or her devastated father.

"I'm going out. Can you grab me a basket?" I asked Gibble when we hit a slow period. He didn't look up, just grunted, retrieved a wicker gift basket from the top shelf, and settled himself in a chair. He would handle the shop while I was out.

I grabbed the basket and filled it with teas—Heartsease, Comfort and some plain old black English tea. I whistled for Lenny and he followed me down the street. We headed to the grocery strip first. I bought some bread and eggs to add to my basket, then set off to Keely's house. When I got there, it was still roped off with police tape. Ernest paced the footpath while Detective Greyson tried to talk to him.

I stopped a short distance away, not wanting to interrupt, but Greyson spotted me.

"You're back?" he asked. "Did you remember something?"

I shook my head. "I just brought this over for Ernest. I... to be honest, I thought you'd be gone already."

According to the local grapevine, the O.C.U. hadn't spent more than twenty minutes at the last crime scene. Come to think of it, I didn't see any of their vans here yet.

Greyson shrugged. "This is my beat. My case." He caught my eye. "My responsibility."

I squashed down the flutter of hope at his words. Maybe – *maybe* – the detective really did have the best intentions, but his superiors wouldn't let this fly. Not for long.

I held out the basket, eyeing Ernest. He'd slunk over to the steps, huddled against the wall as he stared into space.

When I'd found Keely's body he had come rushing in a moment after Lenny. The shock jolted him from his drunken stupor, but was quickly replaced by a grief-stricken fugue.

"Lattersby Street Teas?" Greyson lifted a box and read off the label. "For grief and despair. Steep in warm water for three and a half minutes. No more than three cups daily."

"They're enchanted," I explained. "I sell them."

He lifted another. "What's this one for?"

"Drinking," I said. "That's just normal tea."

"Ah." He carefully put it down and waved me past. "Be my guest," he said.

Timidly, I approached Ernest. "Mr... um, Ernest?"

He didn't respond, just stared past me.

"I brought you some tea." I set the basket down on the step beside him. "Some bread, too. I thought it might help a little."

"You think I'm an addict?"

His words made me jump. I looked up nervously.

"I saw the box," he said, voice flat. "Old Ernie. Pisshead. Not fit to look after his own kid."

I opened my mouth but words escaped me.

"You're right," he said, pushing off the wall. "I am a pisshead. 'S my fault she's dead. Should'a looked after her better." A tear leaked down his face. "She was a good kid."

"She was," I agreed, and scurried away. His grief sent a shiver of sadness down my spine, but I didn't know how to respond. After all, Keely and I had never been close.

Greyson snagged my elbow as I passed him outside.

"I really am sorry about your friend," he said. "And I'll make sure old Ernest there gets some help."

"Can you tell me anything?" I asked. "Do you know who it might be?"

"I'm sorry, I can't." Greyson schooled his expression.

"Look, you know as well as I do that the Talented community outside the walls is being hunted." The anger I thought I'd pushed away resurfaced. "The Lords in the City don't care. The police—no offence—can't handle this. There's magic involved and no-one seems able to protect my people."

"It's a police matter. We've got it under control."

"Yeah?" I asked, forcing him to meet my eyes. "Tell that to my corpse when you find it."

Greyson lurched forwards. "You've been threatened?"

I laughed caustically. "The guy who did this? He's threatening *all* half-bloods. We don't know who's next. We don't know when he'll stop, or if he ever will."

I shook my head in frustration and started to walk away when he called after me. "Lattersby Street, was it? I might drop by sometime. You know, for tea?"

I didn't stop.

CHAPTER FOUR

G ibble was swamped with customers when I got back. I jumped behind the counter to help and had the rush under control fairly quickly. Most days I only opened the store until two, but it was closer to three when I finally closed the door.

Gibble sighed and settled back into an over-sized chair in one corner as I tidied up. He pulled out a small book, thumbing through it until he found the page he wanted. I joined him once I'd finished, flipping open today's copy of *The Protector*, a local rag that helped to pass news to the half-blooded community. News of Keely's death was on the front page.

It didn't tell me anything I didn't know or hadn't guessed. There were no suspects, no witnesses to the crime. Ernest claimed he'd been unconscious when it happened, and based on the state he was in, I could believe it.

Besides, the killer had magic and Ernest did not. There was no non-magical way they'd found to inflict a wound like that without spilling any blood.

Gibble glanced up from his reading but didn't comment. He knew how I felt. I was helpless and scared and I hated not being able to act.

Eventually, I stood. "I'm going to go and restock. Let me know when you leave?"

Gibble nodded. I went into the office, behind the storefront, and assembled my equipment, taking my inventory, my wand and a pile of new, flattened tea boxes. After a few minutes of preparation, I set to work enchanting batches of tea with various spells. We'd been busier than normal and turnover was up. That was good for business, but it took a lot out of me to keep up with the demand for product.

It worked better to enchant the tea in small batches; the spell seemed to stick better, giving it a longer shelf life. With each small pile, weighed and measured, charmed and then packaged into neat little boxes, my weariness grew. About an hour into my task a hollow sensation gnawed at my gut and a dull ache had formed behind my eyes. I'd need to start working in the mornings before I opened to keep up. It only took me a few hours to recover from minor spell-casting like this, but it was tedious work and the strain built up over time. Still, it was a sign of my growing success so I couldn't complain too hard.

I was almost done when Gibble knocked at the door. Lost in concentration, I waved goodbye and he left.

It was almost a week later that I got a break of any description. It was just after closing time and Gibble had taken off as he was sometimes wont to do, having mentioned a stop at the local book shop. I'd just slipped into the back room to create some more stock when there was a knock at the door.

"Gibble? Is that you?" I called. No answer. I stuck my head out into the empty shop, but there was no one at the door. Nerves fluttering in my gut, I darted over to check it was locked.

Gibble usually did that for me, knowing I'd be so absorbed in my work that I'd forget to check. Today, I was glad he did.

The window looked out on an empty street, so I unclipped the bolt and peeked outside. A fat, yellow envelope sat outside my door. I looked around but not a soul was in sight. I grabbed it and went back in, locking the door behind me. A quick peek revealed the contents and I hurried upstairs to my flat.

I cleared off my kitchen table and spread out the contents of the envelope. Photographs and documents stared up at me, forms, reports, and images of dead people. My initial excitement at having the information I needed was struck down by the reality of what I was looking at.

Five people. I knew every face, every name. Two were friends. One, I'd only seen from a distance, only knew by sight. Two more were acquaintances like Keely, who I'd stop and greet on the street. It broke my heart. A monster was targeting my people and it seemed like no one cared.

Someone did, though. Someone had dropped the envelope at my door, hoping I could help. *Perhaps it was Greyson.* The detective's heavy eyes flashed across my mind. *But why? Why would he share this, and so secretively?*

If it *was* Greyson, he must be at risk of getting into trouble if anyone knew, or he'd have given me more information when I spoke to him earlier. Grateful, I made a silent promise that if he ever ventured into my shop, he could have anything he wanted at no charge for the rest of his life.

I sorted the papers by victim. Keely's file was fatter than the others, and I had to believe that was Greyson's doing. Really, though, the police had very little information.

The mortal procedures used, fingerprinting, DNA, other forensics they'd applied had shown nothing. There was no sign of struggle, no witnesses, no anomalies in the victims' tissue samples. Blood work was absent, due to... well, to the lack of blood to work. *Victims.* I had to call them that; I couldn't put names, names I knew to these horrible reports.

Each of them had been found in the morning, one or two knife wounds and completely emptied of blood. I knew there'd been no blood at the scene, but completely drained? That was... odd.

On four occasions, there had been someone else present in the house. On three—both times when the victim had been home alone, and in Keely's case—the knife wound was consistent with one that was self-inflicted, based on the depth and angle of the incision.

One of the other three had taken the wound in the back, so it was impossible that the victim—Carmel, who'd been a close friend mine—had inflicted the wound upon herself.

Looking at the time, I was surprised to see it was coming on 7pm. I decided to call the police station in the morning and try to talk to Greyson. I needed to get a look at the bodies to see if any magical residue had been left, something that might grant a clue as to what was happening. The shop was only open Tuesday to Saturday, so I had a couple of days free to investigate.

Once I'd gone back to read through each file, noted any inconsistencies and similarities, gone back through to check for anything I'd missed... hell, I almost had the damn things memorised by the time I was done. It felt like something was missing, some nagging thought that I'd overlooked. Not from the files—I couldn't put my finger on it, though. Finally giving in, I packed them up, put them safely in a drawer by my dresser, and went to bed.

I crawled under the blanket, put my head gently on the pillow and let the tears fall, until I sank into a restless sleep.

Chapter Five

I stood in a room—stark, with pale blue walls that made my bones ache with cold. A sharp, unfamiliar scent pricked the back of my nose. There was a small white bookshelf to one side and a rug under my bare feet, thick and luxurious but somehow flat and empty of comfort. When I stepped carefully forward, my feet met cold, hard floorboards. The grooves between them felt rough and the wood sent tiny cracking sounds through the room as my weight shifted, small noises made loud in the oppressive silence. I moved toward the bookshelf, crammed with old books and trinkets that were blurry and out of focus. My brows creased as I squinted, trying to focus but failing. I reached out with my hand. My fingers found an object slipped between two books and pulled it out. It was a knife. Long and bronze, my eyes focused on it in perfect detail—it was intricately engraved and adorned with rubies, with a solid handle and what looked to be a terribly sharp blade. But wait, it wasn't really sharp, was it? It was old and worn with use. Slowly, I lifted it closer to my face to examine the sharp, sharp blade. But, not sharp enough to cut? Surely... yes, it was quite blunt, safe to handle. Deep in thought, I lifted its point to my sternum and pressed it lightly. Oh, right, it *was* sharp. I cocked my head, trying to catch the thought *fluttering by... Caution tickled at the back of my thoughts insistently... something was off... something was very, very wrong.*

Pain.

~

I woke in bed. I gripped something in my left hand, and my chest stung. My head swam as I tried to sit up, but I persisted. Perched on the edge of my bed, I reached out and flicked on my bedside lamp. My hand still clutched the object and after recovering from a somewhat startling flood of light, I saw it was, indeed, a knife. It wasn't mine; in fact, I'd never seen it before. I examined it, lost for a moment in the design on the silver handle. As I turned it, I caught my reflection in the blade which was tipped with a small drop of blood. I watched it fade away, *into* the knife. I jerked as I snapped into proper consciousness, dropping the knife.

My head cleared and everything came back into focus. My blankets twisted around me and I had to untangle my legs before swinging them over the side of the bed.

The knife lay on the floor in front of me and my hand absentmindedly rubbed the sore spot above my stomach. Afraid of what I'd find, I lifted my shirt gingerly to examine the wound. There was a small, bloodless incision below my ribcage. The knife seemed to have missed anything vital—or I assumed so, as I was still alive and, I hoped, coherent.

I heard someone down the street yell for quiet and realised with a start a dog was barking loudly. Lenny? I looked and didn't see him. It sounded like the noise was coming from downstairs, in the shop. Legs shaking, I went to find him.

It took a few moments but I eventually found him locked in my work room. As in, the door was actually locked. *What the hell?* I pointed my wand at the lock and focused a spell on it. My trembling hand mistraced it the first time but on the second attempt it clicked open. I held my wand out like a tiny sword, point forward as I slowly cracked the door open.

Lenny poked his nose out immediately, pawing at me and shoving the door all the way open. A quick tracing lit the room. There was no one there.

Lenny fussed over me gently as I sank to the ground. Confusion welled, drowning everything else out, and I wrapped my arms around my knees as I shook. My mind ticked over, going through what had happened.

There had been the strange, surreal dream about a knife. I woke up to find that knife in my hand, and a hole in my chest. My hand strayed to the tender site. Somehow amongst all that, Lenny had locked himself in a room? Magic was involved here, on a scale that terrified me.

After a while, I stumbled back into my bedroom to look at the knife. It wasn't how it had looked in the dream; this one could almost have been an oversized letter opener. It was solid silver. The blade was double-edged and looked sharp all the way, danger made pretty by the tiny patterns engraved on the hilt.

Looking at it made me nauseous and the patterns swirled as my head spun. Too afraid to touch it directly, I used a discarded sock to pick it up and drop it into a drawer. A comforting snick sounded as I locked the drawer and hid the key in the back of a cupboard.

I couldn't avoid the simple truth—whoever was killing half-blood Talents had just targeted me. Worse, he'd attacked me in my house, in my own dreams. Why had I survived?

As I wondered if any of the others had experienced a near-miss like mine, I realised what had been nagging at me previously. Arthur and Maeve, two of the half-bloods that had died, had both been in to buy a sleep remedy in the weeks before their death. Keely, of course, had placed an order for it too.

What does one do when confronted with a horrifying, confusing situation that one can't actually do anything about? One hides under the blankets until daylight of course. Preferably with a huge, dopey dog to keep you safe until morning.

Sometime after sunrise I woke, stiff, sore and gritty-eyed. Lenny sat next to me, awake and watchful. I wondered if he'd slept at all. A short while later, the smell of strong, freshly brewed coffee permeated every inch of my flat. Despite selling almost every kind of tea known to man, I still had a healthy appreciation for caffeine in its stronger forms. I made it with a bit of extra sugar and milk and cuddled into a throw at my desk as I waited for my computer to start up. A brief search online turned up little, but I'd expected that. My answer lay elsewhere. What to do next?

I wasn't in the habit of calling the police. They had never been particularly helpful with anything involving magic. Still, Greyson seemed serious. I picked up the phone and dialled the local station.

"I need to speak to Detective Greyson," I told the woman, Christine, at the other end.

"He's not in just at the moment. Can I take a message?"

"I need to speak to him about the half-blood murders," I said.

Christine clicked her tongue. "You'll need the Otherworld Crime Unit for that one. Here, hold on a tick and I'll get you their number."

"No," I said. "I need to speak to Greyson. He picked up the case yesterday."

"Oh, that young girl on Pike street?" she asked.

"Yes. Please, I just need him to call me as soon as—"

"No, love, that case was kicked over to the O.C.U. Do you want their number or not?"

I slammed down the phone, the last bit of hope dying.

Thumping my hand on the desk hard enough to hurt, I realised I was caught between a rock and a really unpleasant place. The police had washed their hands of it. The Talented, those high and mighty

Lords who lived in the Inner City? They wouldn't care about a mere half-blood.

As for my own fractured community, we had never had the cohesiveness to deal with an emergency like this. Even if we had, the knife that was now in my possession was unlike anything I had ever seen.

A shiver went through me as I realised the power used to create something like this was out of the scope of anyone but a full Talent. Maybe they *would* make an effort to catch one of their own. Unlikely. But how could I go up against one of them alone?

I didn't want to touch the knife, but I'd have to. I unlocked the drawer and reluctantly picked it up. I took it downstairs into my workroom and placed it in the centre of my desk, then drew the heavy curtains shut as Len settled in his usual spot next to me.

The room looked more like a herbalist's shop, with boxes of tea lining one wall and a bench with the implements I used to pack and label my scribed teas. Clearing away some empty boxes, I closed the door and traced a globe of light to brighten the room. I cleared my mind, then checked the wards surrounding me. They were strong. No energies—magical or otherwise—leaked in or out of the room. Satisfied, I took a breath and traced a spell of discovery upon the knife to find out what it was, exactly. I mean, it wasn't a normal knife, that was for sure.

The spell slipped off it.

I tried again, thinking maybe my tiredness had caused my tracing to fail, but I still had no result. Frowning, I picked it up again to look at it. It didn't *feel* like old magic to the naked hand, but then I didn't have much experience in that realm. I put it back on the desk and tried something else. This time, instead of trying to discover what the knife was, I asked where it had been.

A blurred image flashed into the mirror then engulfed me. I saw heat softened metal forged into a tiny knife. The crackle and pop of a forge rang in my ears. A gloved hand etched a design onto the hilt, a rasping chant droning on, the sharp smell of burnt herbs. A box. I saw darkness, the knife locked away. I waited but it didn't pass. I changed the spell slightly, retracing it closer to the present time and saw the knife again. It sat on my doorstep, yellow streetlights reflecting off its blade. I watched myself pick it up and bring the knife inside and place it in a drawer. Darkness, as the knife was shut away. Next, it was in my hand, pricking my skin. *I remember this. This is where I woke up.*

Weariness flooded my body and my eyes ached as the vision fled. The mere thought of recasting it to fill in the gaps sent pain ricocheting through my head. Stomach roiling, I breathed through the pain until it eased off a little.

Spells like this were unreliable at best and downright frustrating the rest of the time. I'd gleaned some information at least—I'd collected the knife from outside myself, either unaware of my actions or soon forgetting. I wasn't sure how the knife had gotten to my room but I assumed it had made it there the same way. Clearly, there was a Talent who was out to do harm, one who had some kind of power over the mind. That was practically unheard of, at least in modern times. I still didn't know who, or why, or how, or anything else that might actually help me.

Ok, I did know some things. I knew that whatever was happening, it was bad for me and there was a good chance it'd get worse in the very near future.

Though Talent homicides were rare, they weren't unheard of. If the victim was a full Talent or someone ranking in the upper echelons of the hierarchy, it would be dealt with quickly and quietly. Someone like me, on the other hand...

Very few full Talents would associate with a half-blood like me. Relationships between Talented and non-Talented folk weren't outlawed anymore, but there was still a stigma attached to interbreeding because the offspring would often have diluted power.

Of course, we half-bloods were bordering on common these days. Once, mortals had very little power, yet lived side by side with a race of people who could move mountains on a whim. Not to be pinned down, they improvised.

The technologies that existed now were incredible and meant that the mortals could do with machines virtually anything a full Talent could do, and a whole lot more. They'd earned their place in the world and the Talents had always had theirs. Those of us caught between weren't so lucky.

If a full Talent was out on the streets killing, there was very little a mortal police force could do about it without putting themselves at immense risk from the Talent himself, and the repercussions from the Talented Council. The Council had the means to deal with this creep easily enough, but would be loath to spend the resources on what they saw as a stain on their great society.

It said a lot that they'd view a half-blood with less respect than a cold-blooded killer.

Still, it would be worth putting in a report. Some trainee guard might be lumped with the job and if, by chance, the guy was also going after full Talents, they'd be after him like a shot.

With that in mind, I carefully wrapped the knife in a cloth and grabbed my handbag and keys. I went downstairs and into my tea room. Lenny padded along without being told and I was glad of his company.

We exited the store and I turned to close the door behind me, my senses on high alert as I considered the potential for my hunter to simply swoop down on me in the middle of the street. As I fumbled with the key, I looked up to see the reflection of something moving behind me. The warped image drew closer, looming over my shoulder.

I turned and let out a small but focused blast of power, weak but sudden. One man stood there, untouched by my attack, while his friend flew back a foot or two, stumbling to keep on his feet. His arms wrapped around his chest, right where my poorly aimed shot had gone.

Dammit, there are two of them. Lenny's tail wagged slowly as he watched the man stand and brush himself off. The dog was utterly unconcerned. Which meant... *Dammit! I've just whoomphed an innocent guy.*

There was no way Lenny would have let some creep sneak up behind me. I stammered, unsure how to apologise for having socked someone in the etheric gut. Before I could voice my apology, his companion stepped smoothly between us.

The man in front of me smiled and offered his hand. I stared blankly at it while he spoke. "Hello. I think you've just... well, Martin will be ok. Not the first time it's happened to him, I'm sure." He spared a glance over his shoulder to check on his friend. "I'm Harrod. Harrod Umbers. I'm here about... something rather delicate. May we come in?"

By this stage, Martin had shaken himself off. "We think you might be able to help us," he said without pause. "Assuming your reputation stacks up to what we've heard."

He didn't seem overly bothered by the fact that I'd thrown him into the bushes... well, not until he righted himself, then clocked Harrod across the back of the head.

"Ow! What was that for?" Harrod winced at the unexpected attack.

"You blocked that spell. Why didn't you block *me*?" He shook his head, looking disgusted.

"Martin, I've told you a thousand times it's a bad idea to sneak up behind someone with Talent. I can't protect you *every* time you do something stupid."

"Who *are* you?" I interjected. Clearly, Harrod had magic, but that didn't explain a damn thing.

"Martin." He jabbed a thumb at Harrod. "He's Harrod."

"I caught that," I said, bewildered. "But what do you want?"

"It's about the killings." Harrod tipped his head to the door as if suggesting we go inside to speak privately.

I looked at Lenny, whose advice consisted of whumping his tail on the ground. Heaving a sigh, I unlocked the door and went back inside.

"Tea?" I asked as they followed me in. I damn sure needed some. Coffee wouldn't be nearly enough, so I pulled down a box from a top shelf and started adding it to a teapot behind my counter.

I dumped two whole scoops of Cognizance into my cup—whatever these two were up to, I was sure it would take every bit of brain power I possessed to keep up with them.

"Please. Um, English breakfast?" Harrod said.

Martin settled down into a plush armchair across from him as he said, "Perhaps something with a little Talent boost for Harrod. I believe you do another that reduces the need for sleep? I'll take that, I was out all night and I'm utterly knackered."

"Do you want to add the boost to yours?" I asked.

Martin's mouth twisted into something that held a bitter sort of humour. "You'd be wasting it. I'm not Talented."

"Ah." *Well, this day just holds one surprise after another, doesn't it?*

A high-born Talented Lord, which is what I had immediately pegged Harrod as, hanging around an unTalent? *There's a lot more to these two than meets the eye.*

Waving my wand, I heated the water with a spell. I regretted it immediately. The working I'd done earlier had taxed me and I had a headache.

When the teas were ready, I took them over on a small tray. I set it down and settled myself in a high-backed seat.

"Who'd like to start?" I looked at Harrod, assuming he would take the lead. Instead, Martin spoke.

"I'm Martin. He's Harrod. Hmm, I said that already, didn't I?" At my nod, Martin grinned. "Sorry. Anyway, my brother here said you're the girl to go to for the latest rumours, gossip and half-baked theories that are circulating around the city."

I blinked. Apart from their rich sepia skin and jet black hair, there was nothing to show they were related. Martin, tall and wiry with dark locks and a light stubble stood in stark contrast to Harrod, the shorter of the two with neatly trimmed hair and a clean face. A second shock hit as I released the deeper implication – Martin wasn't just an unTalented, he was a null, a child born to Talented parents who, through some strange trick of genetics, inherited none of their magic.

"We're investigating some rather unpleasant occurrences this side of the Wall," Harrod said patiently.

"Yes," Martin said, cutting in. "Half-bloods are being killed, rather gruesomely. The guards don't think it's worth their time to get involved and it's well above the pay grade of our local police. We thought we'd take it on ourselves, bit of a challenge. Nothing like a serial killer to perk up your day, right?"

I gaped at him. "That's..."

"Inhuman? Cold? Insensitive, rude and... what was it Deirdre said? Oh, the intellect of an ogre's pet smaj. And that's not the worst he's been called," Harrod piped up. "Martin here isn't exactly Mr. Congeniality, but he *is* very good at what he does. He does care about the victims, it's just that he doesn't really know how to express that like a normal person."

Martin raised an eyebrow at him but didn't respond. I passed them each a cup of tea, feeling somewhat perturbed. Martin started drinking his immediately, but Harrod stared at his for a moment first. As a half-blood I couldn't see him trace a spell, but I assumed he was checking what I'd done to it. Apparently satisfied he took a sip, then another. After a second, his eyebrows climbed and a soft breath was drawn.

"You *are* good," he said almost under his breath.

"I know," I said confidently. If I knew one thing, it's that my teas were good. *Very* good. Martin was already sitting a little straighter and the tired lines around his eyes were diminishing.

Sucking in a deep breath, I decided to jump right in. "I was attacked last night. I think it might have been a dream stalker; I was on my way to make a report to the guard." With that out, I eyed the two men. They both looked stunned. "What *I'd* like to know is why you're here. You still haven't told me what you have to do with all this."

"Attacked? Gods, we didn't expect that," Martin said.

"That's why you were so skittish earlier?" Harrod asked.

"I'm not normally in the habit of blasting people at my door," I admitted.

"We've been living out here for a couple of years," Harrod explained slowly. "Well, Martin's always lived outside the City... We got to know a lot about the local Talent though we didn't mix with them ourselves. We have a few contacts in the Messenger family, so when Talents started disappearing, they let us know. Just to be careful, I mean. They don't know I'm a full Talent."

"How could they miss it?" My hasty words were immediately followed by a creeping heat over my face.

"I told you, Harrod." Martin sat back and chuckled. "You can take the boy out of the Inner City, but you can't take the stuffy mannerisms and posh words out of the boy."

Harrod scowled, but didn't say anything.

"So, you're a Lord." My patience was worn and I wanted to get the conversation back on track. "What are you doing living out here?"

A Talent Lord living outside the Inner City was basically the equivalent of the Queen of England renting a flat on the lower east side.

Harrod exchanged a glance with his brother. "It's... complicated. Well. Anyway, we filed reports but nothing was done. I'm afraid my name doesn't get me quite as far as it used to nowadays."

"So, why are you *here*." I gestured around us. "In my house, I mean. If you didn't know I'd been attacked why did you want to see me?"

Harrod looked concerned. "We came because you—or your shop at least—seems to be a central hub for the half-blood community. You were mentioned as being a friend of two of the victims, and almost everyone we've spoken to knew you, or at least knew *of* you. We hoped to touch base, see if you'd heard anything that might be of assistance. We certainly weren't expecting to find you had been targeted by the killer."

"Please." Martin's expression sobered and he leaned forward, eyes dark. "Tell us everything."

Reluctantly, I explained the events of last night and everything I'd deduced. I retrieved the knife and placed it on the table.

When I finished, Martin asked a question I'd been wondering myself. How exactly did I survive? Dream stalkers are Talents with a very specific gift. They can enter into the dreams of others and watch, or even control the dreams. A trained, powerful dream stalker can coerce a victim into acting while asleep, creating false surroundings and thoughts that the dreamer reacts to.

It was extremely uncommon and one of the only ways a Talent could directly control another person. Once a dream stalker enters your dream, they own it. Even a very weak dream stalker can prevent someone from waking.

My attacker had been able to make me move, which meant he'd had complete control. I shouldn't have been able to resist after that point, let alone wake myself up.

"Maybe he didn't have complete control," I said, partly thinking aloud. "The things he was making me believe—that the knife was blunt, harmless, that there was no pain—those things weren't constant. The knife was blunt, sharp, blunt again. He mustn't have had a very good hold. He was distracted. Or weak, maybe."

That didn't entirely make sense. If he was strong enough to make my body move, he should have easily been able to control the images and sensations within the dream. Movement was the hardest part—if anything had failed it should have been that.

Martin looked at Harrod who explained what I'd just been thinking. "So, Emma was able to distort the dream?"

Harrod looked at me, worried. "Yes," he said. "And if he's after what we think, that means he has all the more reason to come back."

CHAPTER SIX

Harrod told me all they'd discovered so far. Though much of it was old news to me, he did mention he had been able to gain access to two of the bodies. He hadn't found a lot. The victims were already washed and prepped, destroying any magical traces that may have helped to track down the killer.

One thing stood out. They were all like me. Some small amount of magical talent, most of them using it to make an income. All of us too weak to join the Talented society but just far enough outside of normal society to feel a part of it.

Some were thought to be gifted, which meant they were weak overall but had more strength for a particular type of spell. In Keely's case it was the curse stones she made. It was hard to know with certainty, though, as these people often hid gifts and didn't display their level of strength in the Talent.

Though segregation had ended long before I was born, there were still remnants of it remaining. There had been a time when Talents refused to associate with mortals at all, hence the walled off section of Inner City London. Society was far more integrated now, but the divide still existed. People like myself had one foot in each camp but belonged to neither.

The unTalented tried to stay out of our hair, but also didn't like to take responsibility for us. They'd take our taxes and the skills we offered but we couldn't use their schools, hospitals or services. The mere fact that the police force had investigated was probably only due to the recent implementation of the O.C.U., a new department specialising in non-mortal crime.

The Talented also brushed their hands of us. They didn't want our presence reminding them of the effects of the now-legal mixed marriages and cross breeding. They thought us weak and useless and didn't waste their time dealing with such insignificant trivialities as our protection or welfare.

Oh sure, if we put a foot wrong in the eyes of the Talent Lords they'd snuff us out in an instant, but that was only to protect their own less than stellar reputation. Though factions within the Talented community were working towards equality across the board, it was easy to feel anger towards them as a whole – something I imagined Martin could well relate to.

I sighed and sat back in my chair. There is something surreal about surviving an attempt on your life, then finding out the danger is far from over.

"I have no gifts," I said. "And as half-bloods go, I'm weak. Hell, I've barely cast a handful of spells today and I have a headache."

Harrod looked thoughtful at that.

"He must want *something* from you," Martin said. "Perhaps he thinks you're stronger than you are. We think he's found a way to harvest talent."

"Oh *shit*." My hands clenched into fists as I tried to stop them shaking. "If that's true, he'll take out every half-blood in London and we won't be able to do a damn thing to stop him. He's a freaking *dream stalker!* He must be a major Talent and now he's got the power of five half-bloods. He's getting stronger with each attack and we've got... what, one Talent Lord, his unmagical brother and a weak-as-a-used-tea-bag half-blood?"

I wasn't worried, I was terrified. It didn't stop the heat rising to my face after my outburst. I wasn't normally rude, especially to members of my own little community of magical outcasts. *Certainly* not to a full Talent. I think they understood, though, for neither took offense at my outburst.

"The first few victims were very weak in the Talent and were ill or suffering in some way. He's moving up to stronger half-skills and the last two victims were gifted. It doesn't seem random; we think he's moving on to stronger targets each time." Martin left the obvious unsaid. What did the guy want with me? He looked at me, questioning.

"No. Not me." I latched onto a theory that I had only just begun developing. "He must have seen me at Keely's, that's all. I'm weak, even for a half-blood, and I don't have any gifts."

"What's your heritage?" Harrod asked. "Maybe that's of note. One of the women was African, another was a Scot with a trace of the older Celt blood in her."

"Mostly English. My mother and all her line are mortal, but my father was a full Talent, not highly ranked though. He was a bit on the out with some of the other Lords." *That* was an understatement. It was also only half the story, but I wasn't about to go sharing my family history with a complete stranger. "How many others have been attacked? I only know about the ones who... didn't make it."

Martin and Harrod glanced at each other, Harrod looking uncomfortable.

"Oh," I said. "Not even one?"

"You're the first survivor we've found." Harrod lifted a single shoulder apologetically. "There might be others, but no one has heard anything. We've been tracking this since the second victim. We're trying to get word out for information and to let people know they aren't safe. That was why we came to you."

"Harrod, surely there's *some* way for you to find him. A spell, something!" Desperation laced my voice but I wasn't so proud I wouldn't beg for help.

"It's not working. I've tried." Harrod's eyes dropped to his clasped hands. "The second victim had a bit of a talent for hiding—we damn near didn't see the body until we tripped over it. I think I was close to him soon after that. I mean I'm not sure, completely. I sensed a Talent nearby but couldn't see anyone, you see. It was after that I realised he might have harvested the talent from those he'd killed."

Harvesting, the act of stealing other's talent, was an ancient, outlawed skill that was all but forgotten now. In the past, it had been used to create terrible warlords and excuse the murder of millions of weaker Talents... and quite a few stronger ones, too.

The problem was, these powers were only temporary. They only lasted a few weeks at most, so anyone relying on this artificial boost to power had to top up at regular intervals.

Once the Council of Lords had been formed—originally to take down a rather nasty dictator trying to flatten Scotland, England and Wales under his thumb all in one go—they formed a sub-government of their own to prevent harvesting and the unlawful killing of Talented. If they hadn't, Talents would have all but died out by now.

"The first victim appeared over two months ago," I said. "How long do these stolen powers last?"

"That first lot would be wearing off by now, assuming we're right and that he's using the old methods," Martin replied.

For someone with no Talent, the guy knew a lot about our world.

"Pretty little thing for something so dangerous." Martin picked up the knife and examined it again, holding it up so the light glinted off the shiny metal. He flipped it in his hand and passed it back to me, hilt first. "I think we've done all we can here. You know everything we do now, so take care. If we have any more questions, we'll return."

"What?" I gasped. "You can't just *leave* me here! What the hell am I going to do?"

"Of course we're not *just* going to leave you here," Harrod said. "I'm going to ward your house. I'll give you Martin's phone number, you can call if you run into any trouble. If you can imbue some tea with Dreamstop, that should give you some amount of protection. I'm afraid there's really not much more we can do, but we'll pop by and check on you in the morning."

"We will?" asked Martin, seemingly invisible to my distress.

"Of *course* we bloody will," Harrod said, sounding exasperated.

"Right, yes. Of course we will. We'll see you in the morning then. Cheerio!" Martin headed for the door with Harrod trailing behind him. The Talent Lord stopped to etch a small design on the door frame with his wand, then spent a few minutes tracing a spell as his companion tapped his foot impatiently. Then, they were gone.

CHAPTER SEVEN

The next few days passed slowly. Harrod had returned the knife to me, saying he hadn't been able to find anything of use. He and Martin popped in each morning to check on me, but the wards Harrod had used seemed to be doing the trick. No strange dreams taunted my sleep, and no random weapons were left at my doorstep.

Despite the uneventful nights, sleep was elusive. My days were spent in an irritable funk. Nights, tossing and turning between short periods of unrestful sleep.

On Wednesday morning, Gibble arrived at his usual time. He shuffled over to the counter, then grunted at the already boiled teapot. He didn't like it when I threw off his morning routine. In protest, he stomped over to an armchair, pulled a book from his back pocket and started reading. "That's it, huh? No work from you today?" I said dryly. He just snorted. I left him there and went to open the shop.

My morning stretched out. A feeling of dread had settled in my gut and I just didn't want to be there. The customers seemed to pick up on my mood—even those who would usually stay for a chat seemed to want to get their order and leave.

I wanted it to be quiet so I could disappear and think for a bit, but despite the reduction in loiterers, the day was still busy. There were lots of custom orders for the weekend and a few for those who liked to party (or hunt, study, or whatever else my teas were used for) mid-week. Eventually the sales slowed and the break between customers stretched out to a few minutes at a time.

Gibble was a decent attendant, as long as you didn't give him anything too complicated to do. Normally I tried to stay close in busy periods, as he didn't have the personality for customer service. Today, though, I really didn't care about the damn customers. I wanted to go. Anywhere. I needed to think.

"Emma! Any trouble since I last visited?" Jacoby wheeled past the open door, then released his spell to let it shut gently behind him.

"Oh, you know..." I vacillated. As the only Talent Lord I knew—apart from Harrod, I amended—perhaps he would be able to help. "Just the usual."

He nodded as I closed my eyes, cursing my instincts. Jacoby was a customer, and though he'd helped to avert disaster once, that didn't mean he cared enough to help me hunt a killer.

"You're sure?" he pressed.

As the urge to spill my heart out to him rose, so did Gibble's reaction to the old man. The boggart grumbled under his breath as he gave me a pointed glare. "Yes. Everything is just fine. What can I get you?"

"Just the usual."

I wrapped up Jacoby's parcel, took his chips and sent him on my way. Then, I turned back to Gibble.

"What is *wrong* with you?" I asked. "I could feel your hackles raise the minute he came in. I swear, if he ever hears you growling like that I'll ban you from the shop for a week!"

"Nasty man," Gibble said.

"Why?" I pressed. "Because he's a Lord? I don't like them any more than you do, but Jacoby—"

"No, Lady." Gibble frowned. "Broken man. Something not right. Gibble can't explain." He raised his hands in a shrug.

I sighed, his simple explanation softening my anger. As an Other-worlder, his views on what was good and what was true didn't always align with mine, but he had always looked out for me in the past. "I can't deal with this today, Gibble. I'm going for a walk."

Lenny immediately rose and came to my side, his big, brown head leaning into my hip. He'd stuck to me like glue this week, getting under everyone's feet and baring his teeth at a guy who snapped at me when I made him wait. I guess we were all on edge.

After I'd clipped on Lenny's lead and grabbed my coat, we left. We meandered through the streets for a bit, heading towards the City. I'd intended to go talk to the guards about lodging a report days ago, but as I got nearer my pace slowed. Was there really any point? I railed inside because I knew there wasn't. Frustration and fear warred inside me, and I had no one to turn to. Though I had long been too old to rely on my parents, I wished for the days when my father would come to the rescue.

He wasn't the smartest or most competent person I knew—far from it—but he was Dad. The grown up who fixed things. Now I was the grown up and I didn't have the faintest clue what I was supposed to do. I was lucky to even have Lenny and Gibble.

Gibble was a family heirloom, a boggart that was bound to our family for so long that he'd started serving them, for lack of anything else to do. Oh, don't get me wrong, if I left the milk out for even a moment he'd sour it, and things often weren't where I had left them.

He played the odd trick to keep up the appearance of being a malevolent deity but in reality, he was happiest sitting in a big chair with one of his little books. Gibble worked at my shop in return for peace and quiet when it was closed. He vanished at sundown and turned up sometime the next morning—rarely at dawn, but usually before it got busy. He'd often spend his days off curled up on the window seat like a big, ugly cat.

It was a complex relationship, but we were family.

I wandered. Up past the Wall, past the guards who protected those with 'enough' magic and disdained us lesser folk. I hated them in that moment. Until now it had never bothered me, but I knew that with their help I could be safe. Again, I was pulled to speak to them, lodge a report and beg for protection.

Then, I remembered a rumour from a while back, about a half-blood who was being harassed by a Talent Lord. She'd asked for protection and when it was denied, she'd stood at the Wall, screaming obscenities until they'd arrested her. After keeping her for three days, they'd dragged her back to her house and warded her inside, leaving her at the mercy of the Lord who'd been stalking her. She had died three days later of 'unknown causes – likely Talent-induced', according to the local police. Perhaps there was more to the story, but... No thanks. I'd just have to figure this out myself. Well, unless Harrod and Martin came through.

I could go inside the Inner City. There was no law against that, so long as I had my papers and checked in regularly. I could try and hire a room at one of the lodges. Being around the Talents might give me some level of protection—they wouldn't want a death inside the Inner City after all—but I couldn't afford to do that for long. Plus I'd have to endure constant looks, questions asking why I was some-where I didn't belong. No, may as well give up on that line of thought altogether.

I turned down another street, heading toward the deli. Perhaps I'd stop for a bone for Lenny. A sort of apology for what had happened. The dog appeared to bear me no ill will after his night locked away, he just seemed worried about me.

When I came back into the shop, Gibble was still sitting in the chair as though he hadn't moved. I noticed a pot on the sink behind the counter, though, so he'd been up to make some sample teas for customers. He didn't drink it himself.

"Gibble, how much do you know of dream stalkers?" I asked.

A hot cup of tea would put things to rights, I hoped. I selected a blend off the top shelf that helped with cognition and making mental leaps.

"Dream masterss? They slippery. Slipss into dreams and make you mad," he said melodramatically.

I just looked at him, tapping my foot. Really. All 32 years of my life and he still thought he'd fool me? I waited.

After a moment, he dropped the 'stupid Otherworlder' façade and heaved a sigh. "Gibble be knowing a little bit. They enter the mind when you be sleeping. They be able to twist the dreams and hurt the seers. The worst ones, they be making the body move. They be making the people do things, bad things. They be nasty, dangerous." He wagged a fat finger my way. "You be staying away from them. The Guardians will not be pleased if the Lady is hurt."

"A dream stalker came after me last week," I said, wondering what the Guardians had to do with any of it. "Your *owner* would be most displeased if he'd succeeded in his task, so perhaps you could share a little more information?"

Gibble's eyes widened. I knew he'd deny it if asked, but he cared about me, despite his protestations that he was simply here because he had no choice.

"Last... Why did you not tell? This be bad, very bad... The dream masters be hard to defeat. They be hard to protect against. The Lady must not be dreaming." He rose, went to the counter and started shoving boxes around on my shelves. He grabbed one out and thrust it at me. "The Lady should be using this one, imbuing with a Dream-stop and Sleepmore. The Lady should be using the warding of protection on the windows and doors and the warding of the harbour on the beds. The Lady must not try to fight. The Lady *must* resist but not fights. If the Lady fights, she will lose. Resisting is the only ways." His anxiety garbled his speech, making him harder than usual to understand.

"Gibble, it's ok. A Talent came by, he offered to help. Everything is warded. The dream stalker might come back, though, and I don't know how to stop him if he does."

"He won't kill the Lady!" Gibble protested. "He cannot, they will not allow it!"

"They?" I asked.

"Guardians. They be having rules!"

The Guardians were Fae rulers with immense power and fickle ways. Oh, they had rules all right. It was doubtful that any included 'don't kill humans and Talented'.

Gibble shook with worry and regret soaked my heart. I stood and cuddled him, but then drew back.

"Gibble, I think he *has* killed before."

He drew in a sharp breath.

"I think it's the same person that killed the other half-bloods," I gently explained. "He left something here and he might come back for it. I *have* to stop him; how can I do that if I can't fight him? What if he gives up trying to get me through my dreams and comes after me on the street?"

"The Lady must *fight*."

"You said I'll lose if I fight." Ok, now he was just confusing me even more.

"Lady must fight in the world, not in the dream. If Lady fights in the dream, she will lose. Lady must squash the dreamer in the this-world. Lady *must* remember this."

I didn't think he'd have much else to tell me and his worry was making it too hard to understand him. He had some knowledge of the Talents, but not a great deal.

"Gibble, can you ask the Others? See if they know of a dream stalker that's been active. See if they know of his identity, his plan or his weaknesses. Tell me what you find when you come back."

"Yess Lady. Gibble be asking." He'd gone back to his poor uneducated boggart act. I sighed and left him to go back to his reading. He wouldn't leave until sundown but I had confidence that he'd do as I asked during the night.

CHAPTER EIGHT

I went upstairs and sat at my laptop, sipping tea brewed to Gibble's specifications. Harrod's wards had worked so far but it wouldn't hurt to double up. My muscles drooped and my limbs were heavy; the tea had already started to take effect. I turned on the computer and started searching. Unsure where to begin, I looked for anything I could find on Talent murders, suicides, news reports, unusual crimes. Navigating the Othernet wasn't too difficult—I was no expert at trawling for information there, but I'd used it before to source tea suppliers and look for the ex-boyfriend of one of my friends.

Not expecting to find anything meant I wasn't disappointed when I didn't. I mainly looked for chatter amongst the half-bloods, the main users of the Othernet, for complaints about strange dreams or night time occurrences.

There were more mentions than I expected of bad dreams, sleep-walking and one user, 'hornykitty91', who'd had his mortal mum start sleepwalking and attack him once during the night. It had happened just before he'd gone backpacking across Europe.

The dates would place it before the first attack if it had been the same perpetrator. I sent the guy a message, snorting at his choice of username. Having Talent didn't, unfortunately, mean having class, sense or the ability to pick an appropriate pseudonym.

The message I sent was brief—I told him I believed the experience he'd had was occurring elsewhere and could he please get in touch as soon as possible. I hoped he'd do so. The other mentions seemed concentrated within London, close to the Inner City—anything outside this seemed to be more general bad dreams.

Though users of the Othernet didn't give out personal details, I thought I could figure out two of them. One was Wendig, the second victim, asking if anyone had an effective spell for bad dreams after a night of restless sleep. He'd dreamed of suicide, and though he didn't give specifics, I imagined it to be a bad one given his efforts for what was, at that point, a one-off event. This had happened just before his death.

Carmel, I knew immediately from her username—one night, after a dinner party with friends, we'd tried to use magic to create caramel flavoured popcorn. The mix had exploded, coating the entire kitchen in gloopy brown syrup and starting a small fire. Since then, she'd taken up the handle 'CaramelFlambe' in her online dealings.

I was ready to shut down the browser when I noticed something. Carmel, amongst her regular posts about everything possible under the sun, had mentioned her housemate's sleepwalking tendency. That wasn't what caught my eye as I knew Melanie had started rousing during the night a few weeks before Carmel's death. Carmel had come to the shop to request a Sleep tea for her roommate.

No, what caught my attention had nothing to do with sleep or bad dreams... it was the knife. Melanie had woken one morning with a scratch on her leg. She'd found a strange knife in bed with her. Neither of the women recognised it. Carmel had intended to show it to someone—she didn't mention who—but had died two nights later.

It was the same knife, it had to be. I scrambled for the police files and went through Carmel's with a fine toothed comb—no mention of a strange knife at all. They'd catalogued those in the kitchen and a craft knife found at her house, but none of them fit the wound left in her back. I checked the time—it was late, but not terribly so. I decided this couldn't wait.

I grabbed my boots and a coat, slipping the knife in one of the pockets. I paused at the door, looking back at the happily prancing dog.

"No boy. I'm sorry, you can't... no! I'm going to... Oh, for goodness sake!" I went back to grab Lenny's lead and clip it on. He wagged his tail and happily followed me out into the freezing weather. I only lived a short distance from the port-gates and once through, it was about a twenty-minute walk to where I had to go. We traipsed through the streets, cold wind whipping around us in the dark until we reached Carmel's house. The lights were on, so I knocked at the door.

CHAPTER NINE

For a mortal, Melanie had always been very welcoming of Talented and half-bloods. I'd asked her about it once and she said it was because of her wheelchair. No stranger to being treated like an outcast herself, she'd quickly identified with the ostracised half-bloods. I'd met her a few years ago when she came to my shop, looking for a reference for Carmel. She was an exuberant, kind person, always ready for a laugh and deeply caring of her friends. We'd often spent time together, the three of us. Tonight, she didn't seem as friendly.

"Hello? Oh, Emma. It's you."

"Hi, Melanie. I'm sorry, I know it's late but I was hoping we could talk?"

"Well...." Melanie opened her mouth to grasp for an excuse, but I wasn't feeling generous.

"Melanie, I think I know what happened to Carmel."

Terrified eyes shot up at me and she tried to close the door. Dammit, I'd scared her.

"Please," I begged. "He's after me, too. I need your help!"

I pushed against the door as Melanie stopped protesting and wheeled her chair out of the way. It swung open to reveal an absolute mess. Drawers were emptied, cupboards hanging open.... How could she even navigate through this mess?

"What happened?"

"The police," she said quietly. "They wrecked the place when they were searching it. They went through everything."

That had been weeks ago but I didn't say that out loud. Melanie looked so different from how I'd remembered her. She looked... broken.

Her hair was limp and her clothes hanging looser than normal on her small frame. Dark circles under her eyes hinted at sleepless nights and her flat voice made my heart break.

I hadn't seen her since Carmel's death. I'd been selfish, unwilling to put myself through the grief, not thinking of how she would feel losing an even closer friend. What I hadn't realised at the time was her feeling of guilt. Gods, I'd really screwed this up.

I cleared a spot off the sofa and sat next to Melanie. She watched carefully as I took out the knife and set it down on the coffee table. The blood drained from her face.

"Where did you get that?" Her voice was strained and she gripped her skirt tightly.

"It... well, it just kind of appeared in my house. In my hand, actually. I tried to kill myself with it in my sleep."

Melanie gasped out a sob, then pressed her lips tightly together as she twisted her hands together.

"Melanie whatever happened that night isn't your fault." I reached out and placed my hand on hers. "It *wasn't*. Someone is out to get the half-bloods and you couldn't have done anything to stop them."

Tears dripped down her face but she sat still, rigid. "There was no one else home, Emma. I woke up and I knew, I knew something had happened. The knife was mine—I think it was, it was in my bed when I woke up one morning. When I found her I knew, I *knew* it was me. I did it. I killed—" her voice choked off the last words.

I leaned forwards. "It's a dream stalker, Mel. He's a Talent, a powerful one. He controls people while they sleep—I couldn't fight him, and I have talent. It's not your fault. You couldn't have stopped him."

Melanie sobbed quietly. I put my arm around her and told her what I knew, paring it down to the basic details. She'd spent the last weeks thinking it was all her fault. She hadn't known about the other deaths, and it seemed to help when I told her.

When I asked about the knife, she just shook her head, denying any knowledge of where it had come from. I showed it to her again and she blanched away. When I questioned her she couldn't tell me much—just that it was evil, and somehow involved in Carmel's murder. Curious. Then, something else hit me.

"Mel, Carmel said you'd been sleepwalking?"

"Mm. She mentioned to me, asked if I'd take one of your teas." Melanie still had a distracted look.

"Mel, don't take this the wrong way but..." I paused, hoping she'd fill in the gap. She didn't. "Melanie, you can't walk."

"What? Oh. Right. I... guess I wasn't really walking; I was in my chair."

"You mean you got out of bed, into your chair and went into Carmel's room, all in your sleep?"

"It sounds a bit weird, I guess. I'm sure it can happen, though, right?" Melanie squeezed her eyes shut. "I'm such an idiot, of course it can't. I should have known something was wrong, Emma."

Melanie had taken the sleeping tea every night until Carmel's death—apparently, it hadn't worked.

My standard herbal sleeping tea wasn't designed to ward off psychic attacks. Gibble's formula would have been a lot better, had I known what was going on, but I didn't mention that to Melanie.

I stayed a while and begged her to come back with me to spend the night somewhere safe—and clean. She'd completely broken down since Carmel's death, drowning in grief and self-recrimination. I hated that. Could I have helped, if I'd come by sooner? I gave myself another mental kick for not doing so.

Melanie eventually settled enough for me to leave. She refused to leave her home and I didn't trust myself sleeping outside of the wards Harrod had set for me at home. When I left, I promised to return in the next couple of days to check on her and pass on any information I could about the killer. Mentally, I added, 'as long as it was safe'.

Melanie had suffered enough—she was one of the few unTalented who'd embraced the half-blood community and she was put through this. I was sad and angry on her behalf. I hugged her farewell at the door, making a mental note to rustle up some help to send over for a day. A couple of piskes or brownies would have the place righted in mere hours.

By the time the cottage door closed behind me, leaving me alone on the empty street, it was well past midnight. Shaking off my weariness I rubbed Lenny's head and we set off for home.

Chapter Ten

There were only a few blocks to go. Glad I had Lenny with me, I walked briskly, trying to quell my nervousness. This was London, and the City Wall was within a stone's throw from my path for most of the journey. Still, as I walked it was hard not to worry. Feeling overly conscious of the knife in my pocket, I wondered if its owner had a way to track it. Lenny picked up on my anxiety, whining and burring up at every tiny noise.

Lenny stopped and growled, raising his hackles. He sniffed the air once, then continued on. *That's not at all nervewracking*, I thought dryly.

We hurried along, one hand hidden in my pocket griping the knife, wand clutched in the hand leading Lenny. We turned left, then right. Right again, pulling Lenny with me. Wait...

I didn't recognise this street. Confused, I stopped and looked around. This area was one I walked often, there was no way I could be lost... was there? It must be a trick of the light.

Looking around for a building or house I recognised, I saw the street was filled with cookie-cutter houses, none of them standing out in the washed-out moonlight. Tiny, quick puffs of steam clouded around my mouth as I breathed. I raised my wand, calling for light... nothing happened. What? I was scared, that's all. I took a deeper breath, and concentrated, visualising the word to make light. Still nothing—I could feel the slight drain of magic but it didn't manifest.

Even a heavy dose of nerves should have at least caused a flicker or a pop. It was only *light* for crying out loud.

I walked back to where I thought I'd entered the street, but the houses continued on unbroken. My head whipped around, searching for a side road I may have entered on. Tall, dark houses loomed around me.

There was an alleyway up ahead—maybe I'd gotten turned around in my panic. I forced myself not to run, but I was trotting by the time I got there. Blackness surrounded me as I turned the corner, buildings on either side of me blocking out the moonlight. I faced a dead end. As I shook my head in disbelief, I heard a rustling behind me. I slowly turned, heart racing.

There, at the end of the alleyway, was a giant, slavering dark hound. Its glowing blue eyes spat fire at me, and big, sharp teeth bared to let forth a menacing growl. Slowly, I backed up against the building behind me. I looked down for Lenny—he wasn't there, and the leash I'd gripped in my hand moments earlier was gone.

"Lenny?" My voice wavered as my eyes darted around.

He was right beside me moments ago. Where had he gone? And where the hell had this monster come from?

I raised my wand again, trying to conjure up light. Dark hounds had poor day vision so maybe a bright flash... no. I tried again, this time, a push of wind. Still nothing. My mind stumbled, trying to make sense of the situation. Heart racing, I itched to run but the beast blocked my only way out. I held my useless wand out with one hand, then thrust forth the other, holding the knife. The hound took a few steps toward me.

"Back." My voice choked with fear. I coughed and tried again. "*Back!*"

It didn't work. Half-baked plans raced through my mind—run? No way out. Hide? No chance. Magic? Wasn't working.

Lost, alone and terrified, I tightened my grip on the knife, pulling it a little closer to my body. If the beast jumped at me, I'd have to stab it. My stomach roiled at the thought.

I looked at the walls on either side again, hoping for a window or a light. There was no sign of life.

My addled brain knew that was wrong. Even at this hour, people would be awake, especially in this district. My mind turned to how I'd become lost. The dark street, the missing turns... *Oh, shit.*

The dream stalker had me. I was out, away from my wards, and tired beyond belief after my emotional discussion with Melanie. I had no way to tell dream from reality.

My breath came in short, panicked gasps as I tried to focus on what should be. I should be in London, on a familiar street. There should be lights on. Lenny...

Lenny should be with me. He'd never leave my side. I called him, voice wavering. He didn't appear. How did I fight a dream? Would it even hurt me? Ok, I knew the answer to that one—if I was injured by one of the dream stalkers creations it would come through in my waking life... assuming I lived to wake.

I turned the knife over in my hand again, still ready to thrust it at anything that approached. If I had to, I'd fight to the death.

Then, I remembered.

Gibble had told me *not* to fight. He'd told me not to fight the dream, to resist but not fight. I still didn't understand what that meant but I knew I had to trust him. Those damned Otherworld creatures *really* needed to learn to be less cryptic.

I coughed again to clear my throat. "I know that I'm dreaming, asshole," I called to the darkness. "I know what you are. Hell, my dog's probably ripping you to shreds about now."

One could hope. The hound in front of me growled and started advancing towards me. It took every ounce of self-control not to move. I faced it.

"You're a dream," I told it. "You can't hurt me."

As it picked up pace, I faltered. As it came on me, my nerves gave out. Thrusting out my wand uselessly, I couldn't even form a spell tracing in my mind. The creature tensed, ready to jump and I dropped to the ground.

I curled into a ball, covering my face, forcing every bit of power I had out around me by pure instinct.

"You're a dream!" I screamed as it gently snuffled at my armpit... as it... *what?*

I looked up to find Lenny nuzzling me softly. It was Lenny. Throwing my arms around him I sobbed with relief. A brief look around told me I was in a small street not far from where I'd lost track of my whereabouts.

Two dazzling balls of light hung in the air—both mine, assumedly from my earlier tracings. Scooping up the knife, I skittered back against a wall so I could regain my sense of direction. I sat there for some time, trying to work up the courage to leave. Finally, I was tired enough to admit defeat. I wanted my safe little house, my warm bed and my super-strength wards around me. Forcing myself to my feet I grabbed Lenny's leash and set off home.

CHAPTER ELEVEN

I was almost surprised when I woke in the morning, alive and well. Eyes gritty from lack of sleep, I dressed slowly and went downstairs.

After I tidied up the shop I made coffee—double strength, to make up for the lack of sleep. Waking early was an ingrained habit, but I rarely stayed up late. I unlocked the door, Lenny taking his spot near the front as the first trickle of customers showed up.

Pax came in and I made a point to take him aside and let him know what had happened. He promised again to pass on any information he came across and said he'd tell my story to Tox as well. He offered to ask around for a goblin—they often hired out as security guards.

Making up an excuse, I declined. Goblins were one of the few Otherworlders that made me really uncomfortable. It was part of their charm.

Other than that, the morning was fairly routine—lots of sales and a few orders picked up for the weekend.

Harrod and Martin came in just as I was closing. I bade them sit and put some water on to boil. Today, Harrod asked for his own.

English breakfast, no surprises. Martin wanted a physical stamina blend, I had to rummage around for that one.

"Are you sleeping, Emma?" Martin asked. "You look awful."

"Wow Martin, no wonder you're such a hit with the ladies. And no, I hardly slept at all last night..."

I told them both what had happened and passed on what I'd learnt from Melanie. I hadn't gained much that we didn't already know, except a little insight into how the attacks worked. Even that didn't help much—when you couldn't tell the difference between reality and a dream, how could you know what you're fighting?

I asked the men what their plan was.

"I have some contacts I can get in touch with." Harrod didn't elaborate but I guessed they must be high-ranking Talents. "There might be rumours of old magic. That's not the sort of thing to go unnoticed in the Inner City."

Martin wanted to revisit the crime scenes but they'd been shut down by the police—who, though doing a very good job of keeping the public uninvolved, didn't seem to be doing much else. They were apparently toying with the idea of visiting a local seer to see if they could shed some light on the situation, but apart from that were at a dead end.

I asked how much information the general half-blood public had. They weren't sure, but it had seemed most of the information being passed around had originated with me, that was why Harrod and Martin initially contacted me.

It surprised me to realise what a key part I had in the community. I'd known that I had a lot of contact with the half-blood community due to the popularity of my teas... I'd just assumed everyone else did too. I agreed to take a more proactive stance about spreading the word.

We agreed that everyone at least needed to know which wards to use, and I'd already started making a stockpile of Gibble's protective tea for anyone who thought they might need it. Harrod said he'd send a couple of brownies my way to help make up more tea, and to scribe the information that needed to be passed on. Though I could print out the human version, the Otherworld creatures would only read it if it was handwritten, and I wanted them—well, the friendly portion—aware of what was happening too.

Martin stood and headed for the door, but I held Harrod back a moment. "The brownies—do you mind if I send one over to Melanie's for an hour or so? It'd be a big help."

"No, no of course not. Look after your friend, you can have them as long as you need."

Martin pushed open the door, just in time for Gibble to pass through, harrumph at the two of them and start cleaning up the counters.

Harrod gaped. "What is tha—No... No, that's... That's a *boggart!*"

Martin stood there, looking smug.

"It's not... I mean, it's not *possible...*" Harrod's eyes darted between me and Gibble. "He's cleaning your damn counters!"

"He's perfectly harmless," I said. "He helps me out around the shop. He's very well trained."

"He... helps you in the... Oh dammit." Harrod looked downright discombobulated.

By this time, Martin was grinning ferociously. "You didn't believe me," he said. "Was I right? Oh, don't be silly. Of *course* I was right."

Harrod glowered at him. "Like a bloody four-year-old, you are. Next, you'll be dancing around singing 'I told you so'. Go on, get it out."

"Your discomfort is perfectly adequate, thank you." Martin turned to me. "Your friend has become somewhat of a legend in the Talented community. Not that everyone believes it. Of course, I'd never repeat an unsubstantiated rumour, would I Harrod?" He held a hand out toward his brother and waited expectantly.

Harrod handed him a bank note. "Hurry up," he said testily. "We have places to be."

"Wait a moment," I said. They both paused and I asked Gibble what he'd found last night.

"Hhhhaaaa. I'ssss findss many badsss Laydeee." I put my hands on my hips and raised my eyebrows. Gibble's eyes turned toward the men. Martin had a hand over his mouth, trying to hold back a chuckle. Gibble hissed at them. He looked back at me and I didn't move.

"Gibble. This is important. Please?"

Gibble glowered at the men. I glared at him.

"Lady... trusssst?"

"Gibble..." There was no mistaking the warning in my voice this time. It usually worked, despite that fact that I had absolutely nothing to threaten him with. Gibble finally heaved a sigh and dropped the act.

"I did find a thing, Lady. There be a cursed one, a Talent feared by many of the Others. One did say to me this Talent be finding an artefact, and that it be a danger to the this-world if he be using it. I did not be told what the found thing was, or where it be found."

"Anything else?"

"Lady, they be scared of the one. They not be liking to tell me the things they did tell. Lady must be watching. Always watching, Lady must be staying safe." He looked over his shoulder at the two men standing behind him. Both looked dumbstruck. He hissed again, then loped upstairs, no doubt to read a book until they'd gone.

Gibble's tale had more than shaken me. I knew little of the Otherworld denizens that didn't venture into our world, but they certainly had more power than most. If they were scared...

"So," I said to the men, both still standing and staring at me. "Any idea what this artefact is?"

"You have a boggart." Harrod sat back down with a thump, eyes wide. "He works in your shop, and you send him running *errands*. To the Others. Anything else you'd like to mention? Got a dragon in your bedroom? What about a legion of dwarvish soldiers that go buy your paper every morning?"

"Oh, it's not as good as it sounds. He's been in the family for, oh, a hundred years?" I couldn't resist a giggle at Harrod's awestruck face.

"He started off as a run of the mill trickster," I explained. "Though, not a particularly nasty one. I mean, he only stole a *few* kids, and they were all found by sundown. Until great uncle Morton. Took them 3 days to realise he'd been left on the roof. The story goes, Uncle Mort just spent the whole time hanging up there with Gibble, reading to him."

"Reading?" Harrod whispered in a hoarse voice.

"Yup. Mort's mother gave Gibble hell when he was found, and after that he just sort of... started being nice. As long as we give him plenty of books to read, he stays out of trouble. He's not very reliable and to be honest, he scares away a few of my customers. And," I added, "if you think I could afford the upkeep on a dragon, you haven't seen my bank account."

Harrod just shook his head.

It really wasn't a big deal; I'd known Gibble all my life. As long as I kept him well-supplied with books he didn't bother me, despite my father's pleas for Gibble to keep me out of trouble.

As I got older, I would trade the books for favours. It was a run of the mill business relationship—as long as you were used to doing business with Fae creatures that were bound to your family for a century, and who spent the hours after dark chilling with beings from the Beyond.

Martin's phone beeped. He looked at it, then spoke to Harrod.

"We have to go." I looked at him, worried. "We'll let you know more as soon as we can." The two men strode out, leaving me alone with my fears. There was a tap at the door and I looked up to see a regular customer waiting out the front, trying to see if I was still open.

I sighed and went to let him in, but when I reached for the door I realised I still held the knife. I must have been absentmindedly playing with it. Disturbed, I slipped it into my pocket, meaning to put it somewhere safe as soon as I was done.

Chapter Twelve

The next day was a flurry of organisational overdrive. Two brownies arrived as promised, waiting brightly outside my door at the crack of dawn. I set Tyn to work blending tea while Gibble unpacked boxes of fresh stock and stored it away safely. I took the other brownie, Pymb, to see Melanie. When I got there, I was surprised to see she'd already gotten to work, clearing most of the mess that the police had left in the tiny house. Still, she sagged with relief when I told her why I was there.

Though she protested, I insisted I didn't need the brownie's assistance for the day and set him to work scrubbing the place from top to bottom. I versed Melanie in the rules—not to thank it, but to leave out a bowl of milk and bread in case it got hungry. Though I considered it briefly, I didn't mention the previous evening's misadventure.

I stayed for a short while, helping to sort some of Carmel's things into boxes. A few were Talent-made and Melanie was hesitant to touch them. Rightly so, as one of them was a warded box that would have knocked her out cold if she'd picked it up wrong. Harrod would know how to find out if Carmel had family to collect the belongings, but she'd never mentioned anyone to me.

The Council was legally entitled to anything that was left unclaimed. Once I was satisfied there was nothing dangerous left for her to deal with, and that she was comfortable working with Pymb's help, I left for home. Despite it being broad daylight, I regretted leaving Lenny at home. I walked quickly through the streets and took a different way back than I had the night before. It wasn't until my little shop was finally in sight that I breathed a sigh of relief.

Saturday was our busiest day. Though Gibble was fairly reliable during quiet times, I dared not leave him long on a day like this. The afternoon passed with excruciating slowness and terrifying speed. I was eager to do something, anything to make myself safer and I knew spreading the word far and wide was one way to do that. Still, I dreaded the oncoming night. Despite the wards that had worked well so far, my encounter on the streets had left me wondering if I'd ever be safe again. I worked in the shop, serving customers while smiling mechanically, trying not to show how uneasy I felt. Finally, the clock hit two and the last idling customer left. I closed the doors and heaved a sigh.

Gibble was at the counter, his back to me. I collapsed in one of the chairs and sat for a minute, Len immediately coming over to flop his giant body at my feet. Gibble brought a cup of tea over for me. I thanked him, surprised. He didn't usually take the initiative like that.

It reminded me I hadn't bought him any new books lately. Though he was content to reread a single copy over and over, he loved getting new ones. He wouldn't accept money or chips, ever, but was always thrilled with a book.

Gibble had given me a brew for restlessness and I sipped it slowly, trying to calm my mind. I was grateful that so far, I hadn't lost the plot. I was keeping it together, but only just. Last night had nearly undone me.

I was tired, stressed and terrified. I had no idea why a killer was after me and the only people I could turn to for help were two strangers and a boggart. For the first time in years, I felt lonely.

My father had always been there for me as a child, but he was the only one. My two Talented sisters—Aveline and Morwenna—hated me for my mixed blood and shunned me. They'd bullied, hurt and even tried to sell me once.

After Father died, I was no longer welcome in his circles. The friends he'd had immediately lost interest in the novelty of his half-blood daughter, and without his power to keep me safe, I couldn't stay in England. I was shipped off to Australia, a country of liberation to some degree. There was less of a split between the Talented and the not, and half-bloods weren't quite as ostracised there.

Still, I didn't feel at home. As soon as I was old enough, I packed my bags and fled back to England. Though far from the elite circles of Talented I'd once been a part of, I'd found my place in society, that of the eccentric half-blood tea-maker. I'd made a network of friends, some mortal, some half-blood and some Other. I knew a few of the Talented who lived outside the City Walls—these were the ones who'd either shunned the society or were on self-imposed humanitarian missions, slumming it with the less powerful.

I settled back in my chair, wondering what to do next. Was there anything I could do? Martin and Harrod were off following their own leads but I had none of my own. I'd done what I'd promised in getting a list of Talented in the area, though most seemed unperturbed by the warning.

My head spun and I pressed a hand to my eyes. Perhaps I should still lodge that complaint with the guard... *I'll do it now.* I needed the paperwork. Where had I left it? That's right, in my study. I stood and headed in that direction.

Crack.

My eyes jerked open. My head rang and I felt like someone had lobbed a bag of rocks at me. I groaned, tried to work out what on earth had just happened and why I was sprawled on the floor. What? I'd been... that's right, I was about to leave on an errand, I couldn't remember what. Now, I was lying on the floor downstairs with a rather apologetic looking boggart dusting himself off above me. My head hurt, I was in pain and I felt ill, so I stayed down.

"Sorry Lady. You should not be sleeping without the wardings. You did be walking out the door and I did think you did not be knowing."

I sure as hell *not* be knowing, but a glance up showed I had, indeed been headed in the wrong direction. I hadn't fallen asleep, had I?

I moved then cried out as searing pain shot through my hand. Somehow the knife had gone through it.

"Lady, still!" Gibble cautioned too late.

Fighting off nausea and gritting my teeth against the pain, I put my head back down. I pinned my hand to the floor. *Don't vomit.*

I rolled towards the hand carefully, then pried the dagger out of the floor. The tip had only just bitten in but it was enough that it made removing the dagger especially painful. It came out and I pulled my arm across my chest, cradling it.

My hand throbbed and the room spun—probably more from the sight of the wound than the injury itself.

"Lady is hurt," Gibble said mournfully. "Gibble sorry, Lady." He carefully wrapped an arm around me and I leaned against him.

Once my stomach settled a little, I looked at it to assess the damage. There was a deep slit in my hand, perfectly clean and bloodless. Now the knife was gone, the wound gaped a little and blood finally started to well. I swallowed, willing myself not to throw up. Blood ran across my palm and dripped steadily down my arm.

"That is making very bad mess," Gibble pointed out. "Lady can sit?"

"I'm ok," I reassured him.

Gibble brought me a towel and I pressed it to my hand, shaking. He then collected the pristine knife off the floor where it had fallen. He looked at it for a moment, then rammed it into the counter top. It sank deeply—it wouldn't be coming out easily. My reeling mind cursed him silently for ruining my bench.

My hand would need healing. I didn't have the focus to do it myself and the blood was running steadily now. A regular hospital was out. If they gave me any kind of painkiller or sedative, it would leave me open to another attack. My only other option was Deirdre, a minor Talent with a healing gift. She'd moved to the outside to help the unTalented, kind of a Mother Theresa with magic. I asked Gibble to try calling her.

He swooped down and collected me into his arms. I clenched my teeth to keep my stomach from emptying. Gibble deposited me into a chair and I used my good hand to pull my phone out. When I fumbled with it, he gently took it off me, stabbing at the little screen with his fat fingers.

He moved away and spoke to her, using his affected voice and as few words as he could to convey the message. I got the impression he didn't like her either—he seemed to have a thing against most full Talents.

After he was done he sat next to me. He raised his eyebrows as if to ask if I needed anything else. I shook my head ever so gently and he settled into another chair, book out but closed on his lap.

Time crawled as I waited, panic and fear climbing into my throat and choking my breath. *Deep breaths,* I told myself.

It wasn't working—within about a minute; I was starting to hyperventilate. When someone rattled the doorknob, then rapped loudly I nearly stopped breathing altogether. Gibble craned his head over his shoulder then lumbered to his feet.

"Come in, Deidre," I called.

"Thanks!"

It wasn't Deirdre's voice that answered—it wasn't a woman at all. It was Martin. I groaned.

This was the very last thing I needed right now.

CHAPTER THIRTEEN

Right then, nothing could have given me greater incentive to control my emotions than the arrival of Harrod and Martin. Though I'd come to like them both, I realised I was also a little intimidated—both by the sheer power of Talent I was coming to believe Harrod had, and Martin's cocky attitude and ability to adjust to any situation. I didn't know either of them well enough to let my guard down, and to let one of them see me in my current state would just be downright embarrassing.

By the time they came in—I could have sworn Gibble was being deliberately slow—I'd recovered myself enough to save my dignity. My eyes were red and I was still a little shaky but I wasn't quite as close to falling in a quivering heap.

Harrod turned white when he saw the blood. Martin just raised his eyebrows.

"Rough day at work?" he asked. That was enough to allow me to finally clamp down on the last of my emotions. "Who knew tea would be such a health and safety hazard."

"It was just a little accident." I mustered up a tight smile.

Gibble looked at me. If he'd had eyebrows, I'm sure they would have been raised. He wasn't going to let me off the hook.

"I sat down for a bit and must have drifted off," I explained. "Gibble saw me take off and tackled me. Unfortunately, I was holding the knife at the time."

Harrod came over and held out his hand. In my pain-muddled state, it was a second before I realised his intention. Of course, he could heal it. Even with no particular aptitude for healing, a Talent as strong as he was should have no trouble patching it up. I reluctantly gave him my hand and waited for him to begin. He focused his concentration while I waited for the tell-tale chill that would alert me to the working he was doing. I felt it, or I thought I did. It was like it touched my skin, then slipped away. He frowned, staring at my hand.

He stopped and looked me over. "Uhm... are you carrying a block?" he asked. Blocks were charms that would prevent another Talent working on the one who possessed it. They were very hard to find and were exhausted easily, meaning most Talents didn't bother with them.

"What? No, I wouldn't even know where to get one." My hand throbbed.

He started working again but it still didn't seem to be doing anything. He looked about to speak again but at that moment, Deirdre made her entrance. She had a flair for those.

She swept in like a whirlwind, wearing an elegant shimmering dress that was more suited to a dinner party. She quickly spied me sitting on a chair in the corner and came over. She ignored the two men and took me by the shoulders.

"My dear, I'm so sorry I took so long. What on earth happened to you? Come now, show me what's wrong and we'll have it right in a moment."

Martin looked somewhat taken aback by her appearance. Harrod simply sat and watched. I think he was trying not to smirk.

Deirdre fussed over me like a mother hen, plumping the small cushion beside me and resting a hand on my forehead with a dramatic sigh. There was no doubt she meant well but I already regretted asking for her help. Wordlessly I gave her my hand and she examined it.

"Emma, dear. This looks terrible. Why hasn't it been tended? Even a light healing would at least stem the blood." She glanced at Harrod accusingly and he shrugged at her.

She stopped talking long enough to channel into my hand. After a second her eyebrows knitted together and I felt her power touch me ever so briefly. I fought the urge to pull away from the slipping sensation that waved over my hand again and again. Martin and Harrod both watched closely and Harrod frowned. A few seconds later Deirdre dropped my hand. She looked at me in consternation. "My dear, are you blocked?"

I shot a glance at Harrod. "Why do people keep asking me that?"

Deirdre looked at me, exasperated. "Perhaps because it seems you are. I'm trying to heal you, pet, and I can't do that if you're carrying a block. Not one this strong. I promise I mean you no harm."

"I don't have a block! I've never had one." I glanced at Harrod, whose hand covered what I was certain was a smirk. "Anyway, would it even work against the two of you? You aren't exactly lightweights and those things are notoriously weak."

"Clearly there's something stopping us." Deirdre snapped. "Show me everything you're wearing—don't forget hair pins dear."

I sighed, but obliged her, taking off my bracelet, ring and three pins and an elastic from my hair.

"This not be a thing of things. It be a thing of Lady." Gibble finally piped up as Deirdre eyed my dress. I hoped she wasn't about to ask me to take that off too. "Lady did resist the dream stalker, and one other, but that be long time ago. This be Lady's doing. This be her gift."

Silence filled the room as Harrod, Deirdre and I gaped at him.

"Guys, I'm thinking you're all a little more excited about this than I am. Why is it important that Emma has a gift?" Martin said.

"It's not that she has a gift, dear." Deirdre's eyes met mine. "A Talent who can block organically? It's unheard of. If she could block magic... well, that's a little like saying to a rich man, here's a pauper with a bottomless purse. Magic is power. Emma's gift would make that power irrelevant. How do you think a Talent or a Talent Lord would feel to be told they're irrelevant?"

Martin sat back, thinking hard. "And if our killer knows about it, he'll want it very much. Am I right?"

"Guys, stop." I waved my good hand, rolling my eyes at the ridiculousness of it. "Gibble, you have it wrong—blocking isn't a gift. I know, my father made sure I studied the gifts remember? You used to help me carry the books around."

"Gibble remembers, Lady." There was a quietness to him. "Gibble remembers. Lady does not."

I shook my head. There he was, being all obscure when we really kind of needed him not to. I turned to the others. "Look, whatever this is, can you figure it out? Right now I feel like there's a giant hole in my hand. Oh, wait, there is." My short tirade had given me a small burst of energy but it wore off as soon as I finished talking. I slumped back down into my chair, feeling weak but obstinate.

Deirdre checked the items I'd placed on the table for a second time. "It doesn't make sense. It can't be a gift. Blocking... well, it just isn't."

"That we know of," Harrod said. "Clearly she can do something that should be impossible for her. She's not strong enough to touch either of us. She bested the dream stalker and I doubt he's the type to give up easily. She should be dead, and she's not. This is the only possible answer. Besides, it's not like new talents don't exist, we've found three in the last decade alone." He eyed her as if daring her to disagree with him. Her mind was too busy ticking over to answer him.

"Rubbish," I said, irritated at the way he was speaking above my head. "I know those three cases and the only reason they went undiscovered was that no one ever uses those spells. Seriously, how many people need to speak to fish in their lifetime? Talents suffer unwanted magical effects almost every single day. If there was a gift for it, it would have been discovered somewhere near the dawn of time."

"My darling, perhaps you have a ward nearby? Something to keep you safe? I'm sure I wouldn't let any child of mine live in a dangerous place like this without knowing she was well protected…"

"I don't have a damn ward," I snapped. "And even if I did, it would either affect everyone or I'd have to be touching it. Unless someone enchanted my underwear while I was sleeping, I don't have anything that would work like that."

A bolt of icy cold shot through my hand and I snatched it back. Through sheer force of will, I stopped myself from reflexively punching Harrod with a force spell.

"Don't you *ever* do that to me again! For God's sake Harrod, don't you know anything about basic decency?" My face was flushed red and I shook, though not from fear this time.

"It worked, though. You let your guard down while we argued and you let the block slip because you weren't expecting it." Cockiness bled through into Harrod's voice.

"For God's sake, stop being so ridiculous," I said, shaking my hand which was still numb, if not intact.

"Oh, I *adore* this one." Martin turned away from Harrod. "No one ever gets mad at Harrod, he's too damned nice. It's good to have him ticking people off for a change—usually, it's just me."

Everyone looked at him.

"That's it," I said. "Everyone out. The freak show is over, thank you very much for your assistance, now go." I started shepherding them out of the shop.

"Wait, I think…" Harrod stepped back when Gibble stood, towering over him. He turned pleading eyes my way. "I really don't think it's safe for you to be…"

"*Out!*" I repeated, not giving Harrod a chance to voice his concerns. It was just too much. The shock from earlier, the fear, and having two bloody Talents arguing over my head, throwing spells at me like I was nothing more than a lab specimen had done me in. I needed to be alone.

"Come on Harrod, before she throws something at you. I've had that happen and it's not very nice." Martin was taking far too much pleasure in the situation. He ushered his brother out the door, holding it open for Deirdre. As she left, she shot me a worried glance at me before she disappeared.

∼

I heaved a sigh of relief when they were gone. Gibble disappeared moments later—the afternoon sky had dwindled to dusk, so I knew he wouldn't return. I flexed my hand and examined it, rubbing off crusted blood to reveal pink skin underneath. The cut had healed and I felt no ill effects from the injury. I was a mess, though. My arm and my clothes were smeared with blood and it had dripped onto the floor and the chair I'd been sitting in.

I walked over to the sink, wet some paper towels and started wiping up the mess. With shaking hands, I scrubbed my blood off the floor. As I wiped, the knot in my chest began to loosen. Silent drops ran down my face, turning into big heaving sobs. Still I scrubbed.

I hated feeling scared. I hated feeling helpless. I hated being a victim, after swearing to myself I'd never let that happen again. I cried and cleaned until every surface was spotless, and kept going until I'd emptied myself of tears. When at last it was done, I was completely drained.

I sat back on the floor, leaning against the counter. My eyes wandered drearily over the little shop. It wasn't just my income, it was my lifeblood, my connection to people like me. I felt like a part of something here and the attacks on me were taking that away. My sense of community, my security, the contentment I so relished —gone.

I realised I hadn't really spoken to any of my friends since the first time I'd been dream stalked. Maybe it wasn't the bad guy taking away my security blanket. Maybe it was me. I'd shut down, turned inward the way I had as a child.

When my sisters were home with me, I never told anyone about their cruelty to me. I just took it on the chin, fought back as best I could, and tried to pretend I was strong enough to handle it alone. It wasn't about pride or proving myself. I didn't care what most others thought of me. I was terrified that my father would find out, though, and that rather than protect me from them, he would see that Aveline and Morwenna, his full-blooded Talent daughters, were right. He'd realise this child he'd kept, the one he doted on, was just what everyone said—a useless, tainted half-blood, a weakness, a blight on his family name.

Tears kept rolling down my face as I remembered that fear. Oh, how I wished I could go back, tell that little girl to simply trust. Trust in a father's love for his child. Trust that someone who offered her the world really meant it.

It was too late for that, but not too late for me. I needed to start talking again, for my own safety and to protect others. First, I would tell Deirdre what the dream stalker was after, if indeed our theory about the harvesting was correct. Then, at first light, I would corner Gibble and find out exactly what he knew.

I threw the paper towels in the rubbish and bundled it up to take outside. There was a black Bentley parked across the street. A car like that wasn't often seen in an area like this. The driver was inside – it was Martin. He gave me a nod but didn't move. I let out a small sigh, threw out the bag of bloodied towels and went back inside, locking the door behind me just as the last bit of sunlight disappeared. Despite knowing Gibble had left, I didn't feel completely abandoned.

Perhaps I should have felt a bit of resentment at the unsolicited babysitting but I was really just relieved. Despite my lack of Talent, my father had always worked to teach me it wasn't a disability. Yes, there were far more Talented people out there, but I had an upbringing that prepared me for that. I had the benefits of both worlds—enough Talent to make my life a little easier than those with none, little enough that no one saw me as a threat.

If Gibble was right, that would change... at least, it would if people found out. I had to hope the few who knew could be trusted with a secret that even now had put me in danger. But that was something to worry about later. For now, it was enough to know that someone was watching out for me. Maybe I wasn't so alone after all.

I spent the next few hours sitting in my bed, charging a bracelet with Talent. It was something I'd neglected to do for a very long time and I resolved to work on it each evening from now on. Talent pulled from a charged object wasn't terribly efficient and would only give me so much extra time before the fatigue and headache set in, but I had a feeling I'd need every little bit of help I could get over the coming days.

The next morning, I rose early. I went outside to see Martin still sitting in the car, bundled up in a blanket against the cold. He looked up as I approached and opened the window.

"I'm making scrambled eggs," I said.

"Mm? Oh! Oh yes, that would be great."

We walked into the shop, Martin stretching out his stiff muscles. I led him upstairs into my kitchen. He sat while I made breakfast. We didn't speak while I worked, but it was a companionable silence. I loved being in the kitchen and it wasn't long before the smell of rosemary, mushrooms, and fresh coffee wafted through the house. After plating up I sat down across from Martin. His hair was mussed from his night in the car, and tired creases surrounded his eyes. We sat and ate and when we were finished, Martin stood to put the dishes in the sink. He insisted on washing them, so I took up a tea towel to assist.

"Thank you," I said finally. "You didn't have to stay last night. I felt safer knowing you were there."

"Nonsense. You're our best lead, can't have you taken out while our backs are turned." His words implied he'd only done it to catch the killer, but his face softened, suggesting it was a little more than that. Perhaps he wasn't as cold and uncaring as he pretended to be.

"Do you and Harrod have a lot of friends?" I asked on impulse, realising after I said it how awkward it sounded. "I mean, Talented friends. No one seems to have heard of you guys."

He seemed to grasp my real intent and told me that though they had lived in outer London for some time, they didn't know a lot of people. Harrod had only tracked Martin down a few years back—Martin, with no idea he had Talented blood running through his veins, had assimilated into his new life with some trepidation.

His position in the community was extremely rare. Martin should have been like any other full-blood Talent, if not stronger. A twist of fate, however, saw him born without a lick of Talent whatsoever, and his mother, rather than risk her high standing in the community for a Faulted child, immediately passed him to an orphanage and never spoke of him again.

When Harrod's mother passed away he found out the stillborn baby she'd had when he was a child had really survived. He had gone to inspect one of the manors outside the Wall that his mother had bestowed on him and discovered the brief start of a long-forgotten diary. Apparently his mother felt some tiny regret after giving up Martin and wrote out her feelings, a process that only took a couple of pages. The clue was enough, sending Harrod out of the Inner City in search of his long lost sibling.

When the two connected, they'd decided to reside together to get to know each other and make up for lost time. I imagined it had been a jarring transition for both of them, but especially Harrod who would be raised to think of magic equating to a person's worth. "We get along well. Taught each other a few things. We're mostly happy," he finished. Though I had no doubt that was true, I wondered if either of them pined for outside friendship—one new to London and the other on the wrong side of the Wall.

"Is it hard? Between the two of you, I mean."

"Because he's Talented?"

"Yes. Well no, not just the Talent itself. My father taught me the way of the Talented society. I didn't have the training of a full Talent —I didn't live it, I just learnt it. It's so different, though. They're so cloistered, it makes their world view pretty messed up."

Martin stared at the dish water in front of him. "Yes. It's hard sometimes."

"He gave up a lot, didn't he?"

"It took him a long time to accept what I was. It didn't come easily—it challenged everything he knew. He still has moments where I can see what he's thinking, that he misses it... but at the same time, he knows it's all a gilded pile of shit." He dropped a plate in the sink with a splash. "They think the world works a certain way, but it doesn't. We, the normal people, we don't need their magic anymore. We have governments and technology and all the things we relied on them for. They're becoming irrelevant and those who see that are either adapting, or they're running in fear."

"Do you think he'd go back if they let him?"

"Oh, they already did. He was never really shut out, just lost a few people that used to hang off his coat-tails. They're more tolerant now, or they think they are. He goes into the City sometimes, still has friends there. He's—well. There are things on the move on the other side of the Wall, and he's helping them along, in a way."

"How do you mean?" I asked.

"There's a vote coming up," Martin explained. "There's a lot of support for change and if it goes our way, it could mean a complete change of government."

I knew about the upcoming election—it happened every decade or so but meant little to me. For as long as I remembered, nothing had changed either inside the Wall or outside.

Rather than destroy his hope for change, I guided the conversation in a different direction. "Have you been into the Inner City?"

"Oh god no." He laughed. "They'd throw me out in a second if they didn't send me up in a puff of smoke first."

"But you just said..."

"I'm not just any Faulted outcast, Emma." He thumbed his chest proudly. "*I* have a record. A dangerous criminal, that's me."

"What?" I scoffed. "You, a record?"

He nodded. "A Talent came in one day and destroyed a whole section of books. He tried to tell me that they were 'dangerous'. I got a little angry at that."

"Books?" His story was getting more confusing by the minute.

"I'm a librarian." Martin sat back, waited for me to digest the idea that this... well, scoundrel is probably how Deirdre would describe him, was a librarian. "Well, I *was*. When someone came in and disintegrated half a shelf of books claiming they were 'anti-Talent propaganda' I tried to stop him with force. Me, against a Talent. A high ranking one, apparently."

"And lived to tell the tale, I assume?"

"Yes, but for a while I wished I hadn't." Martin shook his head, lost in memories. "Harrod bailed me out but the records are still there. We'd only known each other for a few months and I hadn't expected him to step in, but he did. He never did tell me what happened between him and the guards, but next thing I knew I was let out, dumped on my doorstep with a stern warning to never set foot inside the Inner City again. As if I'd want to, right?

"Right." My opinion of the stuffy, opinionated Talent Lord was improving, if only a little. "What happened after?"

"Harrod showed up on my doorstep, apologizing for all his kind," Martin said. "He asked if I'd give him the chance to make it up. Now, we slum it with the unTalented masses and fight the injustice of the times. Superheroes, really, cementing the hate of our overlords against us and not really winning the gratitude of anyone else." He smiled wryly.

"You have mine," I said quietly. "Martin, I don't have anyone else. I mean, I know a lot of people but none that would step in front of a bullet for me – or spend a freezing night sleeping in a car to keep me safe. I have no family who would help. It seems like you and Harrod are the only people that might actually be able to do something."

He looked at me with sad eyes. His concern pricked at me and I was immediately uncomfortable. *Not like me to share so much.* I smiled brightly to cover my discomfort. "Guess we'd better get on with it then. This guy isn't gonna catch himself, is he now?"

We finished up and headed downstairs where Tyn was stacking boxes on shelves.

"Oh hell." I slapped my forehead. "I was supposed to go and collect Harrod's brownie yesterday. He's still at Melanie's."

"I'll come with you." Martin headed for the door. "Harrod was going to meet me here later but we have some time."

We decided to drive rather than take the port-gate. When we arrived, Martin pulling the car up outside her house, Melanie rushed outside, looking stricken. Her expression faded to relief as she saw me.

"Oh Emma, what happened? When you didn't come back I was so worried, I didn't know how to get in touch. When I saw the car... though, I guess if something DID happen to you, they wouldn't send someone to tell me." She reached up and hugged me hard. "Who's he?"

"I'm Martin, a friend of Emma's. So very pleased to meet you. You're Melanie I take it?"

I looked at him sideways. His demeanour had changed from his normal, irascible self to downright charming. After what Melanie had been through, I wasn't sure how I felt about him flirting with her .Reining that thought in, I berated myself. I wasn't her keeper, though if she expressed an ounce of discomfort I had no qualms about telling him to back off. Looking at her coy smile, I doubted that would be needed.

We headed inside and Melanie insisted on making a pot of tea. I did my best to hide my surprise as we entered the pristine house. The scrubbed floors and spotless curtains were a huge improvement on what I'd left. With Pymb's help, Melanie had even rearranged the furniture. There were two boxes by the door with my name on them.

"We found some more things of Carmel's," Melanie told me when I asked what they were. "I hadn't realised how much she'd squirreled away over the last few years."

"You two were close?" Martin asked in a quiet voice, responding to her drop in mood.

He trailed her into the living room as she told him how they'd met, and how they'd grown close over the time they'd lived together. As if expecting the question, she explained that Carmel's Talent had never caused a rift between them, rather Melanie's fascination with magic had been something they bonded over. Martin seemed surprised at that—because of the history between the two, most unTalented despised anything to do with magic.

Pymb brought the tea over to where we sat. Melanie and Martin seemed to have forgotten I was there. Martin served the tea and gave Melanie a mock bow as he passed her a cup. I rolled my eyes while Melanie blushed.

We stayed for a short while, chatting about general things. Ok, Martin and Melanie chatted. They talked about the trials of living with a Talent, and of trivial things like where the best place in town was for a drink and what bands were playing where. Martin didn't seem at all concerned about her wheelchair—I knew she was often treated differently for it, even by unTalented who were more exposed to injury and disability than those of us with access to Talented healers.

Melanie seemed as I remembered her before Carmel's death—animated and warm, ready to laugh and at ease within herself. I was glad. It eased a little of my guilt for what she'd been through and let me hope that everything—not just this one thing, but everything—was going to work out.

I clung to this hope, even as we readied to leave and I saw Melanie retreat back into herself again. I could understand why she didn't want to be alone. I resolved to visit more often.

As Pymb bounced into the back seat, I thanked Martin.

"What for?" He gave me a quizzical look.

"Cheering her up. She's been through a lot."

"Well, I suppose you can thank me again Friday night."

I shot him an enquiring glance and he held up a slip of paper.

"You got her number? Martin! She's my friend! And she's been deeply traumatised. Don't you go taking advantage of that." I was mostly mocking in my criticism but he took it seriously.

"She gave it to me, I didn't ask.... Oh all right, I promise I'll be careful."

I settled back into the leather seat for the drive home. As we turned the last corner, I saw a cluster of people and cars just past the shop.

CHAPTER FOURTEEN

Martin pulled up into the spot he'd in parked earlier and we hurried down to the gathering. Two cars had parked in the middle of the street and there was a handful of people standing around Gibble, who bent over something in the middle. I pushed through, Martin and the small brownie on my tail.

"Gibble? Gibble, what's going on?"

He turned big eyes to me. His movement allowed me to see past him, to a brown, furred body on the ground. I flew to it, a sob wrenching itself from my chest. Lenny. My poor, beautiful friend. He was lying on the road, broken and bleeding.

"Gibble what happened? Who did this?"

"Lady, I not be knowing. The shop be opened when I came and no one be there. I did see a car and a lady, then I did see Lenny-dog. He be hurt, so I be calling someone to help him. Be still Lady, they will be helping him soon."

"Why? Why was he outside? He never goes out without me, and he NEVER runs into traffic."

"Lady... I do not be thinking a car be doing this."

Gibble said this in my ear in a low voice. No one else heard. A woman paced back and forth looking stricken. When I noticed her, she blanched away, looking sick.

"Did you see what happened? Did you do this?"

"I—I'm so sorry. I was turning and he just shot out, I didn't even know I hit him until I looked back. Oh God, I'm so sorry. I didn't know what to do. This—" She gestured towards Gibble. "This creature arrived and said he'd send for help."

Blood oozed freely from Lenny's shoulder, where a bit of skin was missing. Part of his face was blistered. Blood foamed at his mouth and his breathing was laboured. The bottom half of his body lay at an awkward angle and I could tell a lot of damage had been dealt. I tried to make sense of the injuries but my brain refused to work. The woman behind me kept offering apologies. Apologies wouldn't help Lenny right now. I tuned her out.

Pymb head-butted me firmly and held out a bowl of water. Shaking, I poured it over Lenny's face where it had blistered. Behind me, I heard snippets of conversation "Yes, she made a call… a vet I think." I pressed a towel into the open wound. Martin must have sent the brownie inside for that, and the water. He came over to inspect the damage.

"I've called Deirdre. I don't know if she can help, but she said she'd try. Emma, I don't think this was an accident—" I whipped my head around, searching for the woman I'd seen. "No, not her. Your door was broken and inside is a mess. Lenny might have chased off whoever did it. It would explain why he's out here, at least."

I shook my head, not caring about the shop. Right now, my priority was saving my dog. I took a deep breath and fumbled out my wand. Closing my eyes to balance my core, I started to trace a spell.

"No, ye silly lass! Not like that. He's a dog, not a filthy human."

My head snapped up and I came face to face with a knee-high creature with skin like an old tree. He—I assumed it was a he—hurried into the circle of people and pushed me out of the way. I pushed back with a growl and he looked at me.

"You are his?" he asked. I nodded, figuring it was true enough.

His gnarled face relaxed a little and he gave me a nod. I assumed that meant I could stay.

Gibble ambled over and placed a restraining hand on my shoulder. "Olfred, I be in your debt if you be saving Lenny-friend."

"Ay, ye will be," Olfred said. "It's not often you offer up a favour of yer own, boggart."

"You be doing the work and I be owing you. Do not be failing." Gibble's voice dropped into a warning growl.

The little Otherworlder didn't seem perturbed. "Ay, I know wha's at stake. Now shut ye'self and let me work, Gibble-friend."

Olfred pulled out a small pouch. From it, he removed a long wooden staff topped with feathers and beads. He also took out a bowl of water. Martin made a small sound of amazement behind me.

As incongruous as it was seeing these appear from a tiny bag, it didn't surprise me much. The Others often tread the line between this world and theirs, and sometimes stuff was just plain weird when they were around.

I watched closely as Olfred worked, first touching the staff to Lenny's body, then dripping the water over each wound. A tendril of smoke rose with each touch. Lenny lay still in my arms, rolling his open eye up to look at me steadily. His calmness caused me the most fear—he should be in pain, writhing and whimpering. If the pain had passed, his body was giving up. Tears rolled down my cheeks as I held him.

Olfred, after having touched the staff on every injury, then dragged it around in a circle on the pavement around him. Before he closed it, he paused and looked at me.

"Will ye give of ye'self to let the creature live?"

"Yes," I said numbly, not even asking the cost. There would be no chance of negotiation, not for this. I would give.

He closed the circle. When he smacked the base of the staff on the ground with a crack, everything slipped into a warm fuzziness. My bones ached and it felt like my eyes were being sucked out of my head.

I felt rather than heard the 'pop' that ended it. Air whooshed back into the circle, and everything regained its equilibrium. I fell back, dazed as someone rushed in front of me. Curly blond hair obscured my vision as someone checked my pulse, waved a hand in front of my face and yelled in a muffled voice. I looked up—when had I fallen to the ground?—to see who it was. Deirdre was here.

Apparently satisfied with my condition, she turned her back to me and started running her hand over Lenny's body. As my hearing cleared, I heard her muttering curses—something about 'stupid Otherworld meddlers trying to kill her people'. I had no idea what she meant.

I struggled to my knees and leaned over to check Lenny, mindful of my stomach that tried to empty itself as I moved. Steadying myself, I saw that he was breathing, if asleep. His body was straight and lithe and his wounds were closed. Dry, matted blood still stuck to his fur in places—in others, fresh, pink skin showed where hair would need to grow back. Otherwise, he'd gained a sleek sheen to his coat that looked much smoother than normal.

I sat back as Olfred waddled over to place a hand on my shoulder. "Sit ye'self back now. Tha' will have taken its toll on ye."

Deirdre whirled on him, furious. "What on earth did you think you were doing? A spell like that can be *highly* unpredictable and *extremely* dangerous. You could have taken too much from her. You could have *killed* her little man and if you had, I assure you, you would have had me to reckon with. You will *never* take life from one of my people again. Do. You. Understand?"

"Ah pipe down, ye silly lass. I'm a god—or I used to be one at any rate. A wee one, but a god just the same. A casting like that draws from *my* world. Just because ye can't handle Other magic ye'self, dinna mean those that hail from there canna. Yer lass was safe, I'd not take more than she could give."

He took life? A rush of understanding hit me, making my head reel.

"Deirdre, he had my permission. I gave it freely." No wonder she was so angry—this kind of magic was anathema to Talents and I imagined a healer would have more hate for it than others.

She shot a glance at me but stopped berating Olfred. The last thing I wanted was for him to leave offended after what he'd done, but it looked like he'd brushed her off as nothing more than a petulant child. On Deirdre's part, she was now packing things back into a small bag. She'd arrived expecting to tend to Lenny but it looked like she wouldn't be needed now. She strode over to Olfred and said something to him quietly. Her furtive glance at me suggested she didn't want me to hear what she said, but Olfred either didn't understand or didn't care.

"She's got that dream stalker after her? Ach, why dinna she say? I wouldn't have drained her near as much. She won't be fightin' much off in her condition for some time." He shrugged his lumpy shoulders. "I could have left her a wee bit more, I suppose."

I groaned inwardly. Who had told Deirdre about that? Olfred shook his head at me as if *he* was put out by condemning me to an almost certain death.

"What about Lenny?" I stopped him before he left. "Is there anything I can do for him?"

"He'll be right in a couple of weeks." Olfred waved his staff. "Not the injuries – all tha' has been healed. He just needs to adjust."

"Adjust?"

"Ay. He was bad, very bad. He's lucky I got here when I did. The life I gave him was part of ye—somethin' grounded here to catch his spirit, stop it from leaving. He also got a little from the Other, that's wha' gave it the kick it needed to fix the body. Now, he has both inside. He has to learn to use both and it can be a wee bit disorienting for a while. He'll be hungry, so make sure ye feed him. Let him sleep. After, he might be a wee bit... *more* than ye remember."

I didn't question what 'more' meant. Lenny had been touched by the magic of the Other and that's how he'd be from this point on.

There were stories about beasts who'd been touched like that. Stories of supernatural strength, human cognisance, and flying pigs.

No, I mean actual pigs that fly. One, anyway. Or maybe it was a boar. Regardless, my dog might never be the same again—he might also not change a bit. I wouldn't know until he regained his strength.

～

Around me, people were starting to disperse, losing interest now the funny little man and his strange magic had left. Deirdre helped me to my feet and I was surprised when Lenny lumbered to his. He moved slowly, but he seemed to be back in one piece. I choked on tears, realising that a few minutes ago, I hadn't expected him to stand up ever again. We trailed over to the sidewalk so the traffic could start flowing again. Lenny had held up one of the lanes—the spectacle of an Otherworld creature healing him had held up everything else. Now we were done, people suddenly remembered they had places to be.

The woman who had hit Lenny with her car came over.

"Is he going to be ok?"

"Yeah. I think he will." I turned away but she side-stepped, unwilling to end the conversation just yet.

"Again, I'm so sorry." She wrung her hands. "You won't... Um..."

"Press charges?" I shook my head. "Everyone said it wasn't your fault."

"I didn't mean that... You won't, like, curse me or anything? I *really* didn't see him, he just—

Anger flushed my face. "For goodness sake, have you ever actually *spoken* to a Talent before? We don't curse people." Keely's stones flashed into my mind but I didn't think it was prudent to amend my statement. "We use magic the same way you use phones and cars and medicine. We don't go around stealing babies and withering crops."

"I... oh. Sorry, I guess. I've just never mixed with your sort before." She wandered off, apparently losing interested now she knew the fury of the wicked witch wasn't about to be unleashed.

Seriously, some people. Just as my heart rate was starting to normalise, I heard a curse.

"Damn witches. Wish the stupid mutt had died."

The adrenalin, the fear, the anger. All of it kicked back in at once. I launched myself at the man, screeching. "How dare you? How dare you say that about my dog? He's my friend, He's my BEST FRIEND!" I hit him in the chest, pummelling him with my fists and he pushed me back. Throwing myself at him again, reaching for his face, his hair, I did anything I could to inflict damage. Arms grabbed me from behind, pulling me back as the man flailed, trying to dodge my angry fists.

"Go on bitch!" he yelled back at me, a moment before something wet hit my face. I struggled harder but whoever it was had a good grip. I turned on them, only to come face to face with a stony-looking Harrod.

My movements slowed and my limbs went flaccid. He was using magic against me. Magic! I had just enough movement left to tip my wand in his direction. He must have read my face.

"Emma, don't even think about it. I'd take you down in a heartbeat."

It was his tone more than his words that stopped me. He spoke in a quiet voice, anger behind it tightly controlled. I hesitated and that was enough. The strength sapped from my bones and I slumped. My antagonist seethed but had enough sense to stay back and keep his mouth shut.

Gripping my arm tightly and easing off the Weakness spell, Harrod led me inside. Deirdre had already brought Lenny in. She and Martin fussed over him, the pair parting as I wearily pushed through. Harrod's grip didn't soften on my arm, even when the door shut behind us. Gibble made a growling sound and took a threatening step towards him. Finally, Harrod let go.

Ignoring everyone, I went straight to Lenny and buried my face in his neck as I leaned in for a cuddle.

"I'm so sorry," I whispered.

He licked my face and nuzzled me. I looked up at Deirdre. She was sitting down talking quietly with Harrod, who still looked furious. Stroking Lenny's face, I told him to sleep. He was so tired his head bobbed, a typical after-effect of a healing that strong. He settled back onto the pillow and was asleep in seconds.

~

I instinctively went to the kitchen for tea, only then remembering what Gibble had said. I stopped in shock. Everything was a mess— boxes opened and rifled through, drawers ajar, cupboards open. The register was wide open but the cash was still inside. My shoulders slumped. I knew I should check the other rooms but I couldn't move. I felt so drained. Gibble came up and put a hand on my shoulder.

"Lady is having shock, I think. Sit. Gibble make tea and clean the mess. Gibble make note of any things that not be here when they should."

"Do you have the knife on you?" Harrod asked.

"The knife? No." I answered distractedly. Then, the implication hit me and my hand flew to my mouth.

"You left it behind?" Martin asked.

"Oh sure, I always take a murder weapon when I visit friends," I snapped. "For goodness sake Martin, what do you think Melanie would have done if I'd walked in holding the damn thing?"

I flushed at the cattiness in my tone – and the realisation that I had, in fact, done exactly that just days before, when I had gone to ask Melanie for information about Carmen's death. Martin hadn't done anything wrong.

I went into the study. The shelves in there had also been searched. There was a pile of papers strewn on the floor around the table and on top sat an empty drawer with a busted lock. I returned to tell the others the bad news.

"Well," said Martin, "At least we know the knife's important. Any ideas?"

Harrod spoke but I turned my back on him and started straightening the shelves, refusing to look at him. Martin may not have earned my ire but Harrod... he had used magic on me.

Harrod explained his theory that the knife was a vessel for holding Talent. It was old magic, something not seen in many years. He suggested the dream stalker needed it to siphon off the Talent from his victims, that the harvesting wasn't an innate gift. This added up with what Gibble had told us after his visit with the Others. It was bad news... but also, hopefully, good. If this guy had somehow found the knife and not created it himself, it meant he relied on it—and if we could destroy it, his killing spree would end.

Harrod finished speaking and everyone was silent for a few moments.

Deirdre spoke first. "My dears, this has been riveting but I don't see what we can do about it. This crazed lunatic is stalking the streets, trying to kill half-blood Talents? Surely you don't intend to go after him. The safest course of action will be to bunker down, put Emma into a safe house and make ourselves scarce. Yes?"

"No," I said. "I don't back away from fights." Harrod snorted. "I *also* care about my friends more than I care about my reputation," I continued.

He raised his eyebrows. "Is *that* why you think I stopped you?"

"Come on Harrod, you don't think I know what that was about? You've been taught all your life to maintain that squeaky clean image, and a half-blood punching some asshole in the face would ruin it all."

"Wait, did we miss something while you two were outside?" Martin sounded wary.

"You really think I'm that shallow?" Harrod shook his head disparagingly. "I was *protecting* you."

"By threatening to take me out?" My fists clenched. Screw magic, I'd punch the bastard in the face if he didn't stop talking.

Martin shot to his feet "He did what? Gods, Harrod, tell me you didn't."

Harrod looked at Martin, trying to find the words to explain. There were none.

"I apologise for my brother's behaviour Emma. I thought he'd gotten past that, grown up a bit. Clearly, I was wrong." Martin shot an angry glance at Harrod then stalked out, slamming the door behind him.

"I just..." Harrod turned from the closed door back to look at me. "I needed you to back down. You don't understand. Those in the Inner City tolerate your kind, but if things erupt now, it could ruin everything."

"That's exactly what I'm talking about, Harrod." I threw my hands up. "You're so busy dealing with politics and appearances, you don't know what it's like out here. You live on this side of the Wall but you don't experience it—the hate, the suspicion, the helplessness when something goes wrong. If we don't fight for what's important, who will? The unTalented don't understand us, we're too different. The noble Talents, hidden in their precious Inner City? They don't give a damn either."

"I do." Harrod turned and walked to the door. He stopped for a moment, and I thought he might turn back. Instead, he tugged at his coat, opened the door and strode out, leaving me and Deirdre alone.

Chapter Fifteen

I stared after him, still angry but also confused. His words and his actions didn't add up and I suspected that he was struggling as much as I was to make sense of it. I turned to the one person that might have the answers I needed.

"Deirdre, what was he talking about? The Talents have always just ignored us. Why would that change?"

"The whole world is changing, dear." Deirdre sat back, folding her hands in her lap. "The technology out here has finally superseded Talent. Plots and schemes abound, and though there are more supporters of integration than ever, others still wish there were a way to control the unruly children running free outside the confines of propriety. The Lords feel their place at the top of the hierarchy is slipping; they're becoming irrelevant in a world that no longer fears Magic like it once did, no longer respects those who wield it. Some feel this is in part due to the prevalence of those who flaunt their weakness in front of others, who live outside and blur the lines between those who rule, and those who one day will."

"And you? What do you think?" I leaned forwards, trying to read her face as she answered.

Deirdre had lived outside the City for years, taking care of the half-bloods and offering her healing services to mortals in need—those who'd accept it at least. Still, she spent time in the City and seemed to enjoy the privilege of her rank.

"There is an ebb and flow to all things, child. The students become masters and the children become parents. No one should feel so confident in their place that they ignore those below them. A time will come when the Houses will fall and life behind the Wall will change. Perhaps for the better, perhaps not. Much of it will be due to those outside, though."

"A revolt?" I barked a coarse laugh. "That hasn't been attempted in well over a century. It failed miserably."

"Oh, nothing so catastrophic. It's simply the way of change. I'm doing my part—bringing the pampered children of the Lords out into the world where they can see beyond their walled horizon."

I'd met a few of the children of Talent Lords before and they were all insufferable. Some of the worst were, to my disgust, related to me. I wondered how she could put up with them.

Deirdre rose. "I'd best be off, my dear—I have somewhere quite important to be tonight. All going well, I should return bearing good news on the morrow, if Harrod doesn't tell you first. Now dear, don't pull that face—I know he has a long way to come, but his heart's in the right place. He has a vision of how the world should be —a good vision, one that does him credit. He just has a ham-fisted way of going about creating it. Harrod will watch over you whether he has your permission or not. Safer for both of you if you accept that, and call on him if you need to."

"He's a pig." My anger flared again. "He should know better than to use Talent on another person, especially someone weaker than him."

"He does know better and I assure you, he'll berate himself far more strongly for it than you ever could. Now, your little friend will need close care tonight. Feed him and let him rest. I shall send Martin back to watch over your home tonight. I fear it is becoming dangerous to be you right now. Do promise me you'll take care?"

She hugged me and stopped to give Lenny one last going over. With a croon of satisfaction, she leaned in to let him lick her face, then left.

~

Martin returned a few hours later. He collapsed onto the sofa and gratefully took the cup of tea I offered him. I insisted that we take shifts during the night so he could get some rest, ignoring his assurance that all he needed was a shot of Wakefulness brew—that stuff was great while it worked, but often left its users with the same feeling you'd get after a four-day binge. Of course, many of the people who used it had that exact purpose in mind. I felt sorry for anyone waking up with *that* kind of hangover.

I let him relax while I worked downstairs. The thief had upended boxes, emptied drawers and an entire shelf of tea stock had been destroyed. That would be the hardest to rectify—more than just tedious, the tracings I'd have to apply would need to be done in small batches. It would take time, or I'd end up burnt out. I didn't want to be in a position where I couldn't access the small bit of Talent I had in an emergency. I packed up what I could downstairs. Gibble had already gone through and discarded what couldn't be salvaged and was now doing inventory, so I spent the rest of my afternoon working on my stock levels, checking on Lenny every few minutes despite myself.

I shooed Gibble out of the room so I could concentrate, then set to work. Once the workspace was clear I placed a small bowl of tea leaves on the table. I sat in front of it, feeling its energy and its lines.

Drawing in some of the power I held inside, I focused it into a long thread, weaving magic through the reality of the tea leaves like a flourish of calligraphy embellishing a plainly printed word. Once complete, I disengaged and released the power I'd drawn, ready for the next one.

It really is very simple, not like some of the books and accounts try to make out. An hour later and I was exhausted, but satisfied with my efforts. With Gibble's help, I gave the shop a good clean from top to bottom, a Sunday ritual that was needed today more than usual. Dusted, mopped, scrubbed and sorted.

It took longer than normal because of the disorder from earlier but I was glad I had a chance to sort everything out. Once cleaned, it felt like a taint had been lifted off the walls surrounding me. I hated this feeling of filth invading my home and the ritualistic cleaning had dispersed some of it, though not all. A lingering feeling of unease wafted around and I knew it would be there for some time.

By the time I was done, Lenny was on his feet, if a bit wobbly still. I gave him a bowl of food and took him as far as the footpath out front for a quick trip outside. Gibble waited close by to act as bodyguard before he left for the night. When I came inside, I settled the dog back on his bed and stroked his back until he'd fallen asleep again.

Then, Gibble gone and alone once more, I made some tea. Tea was for thinking, and I had a lot of it to do.

I was angry at Harrod, so angry. Though I understood in part why he'd stopped me, I hated the way he'd done it. Using brute force was how the Talents had run the world for a long time. Descended from a select handful of men and women who had been blessed with their power by the Guardians, the Talented used this as their excuse to shut themselves off from everyone not within their ranks. They'd decided to claim a large plot at the centre of London hundreds of years ago, and forced out the current residents with magic. After setting up a City-within-a-city, the self-proclaimed Lords took advantage of the benefits of bustling outer London, but never contributed to its wellbeing.

It was only in the last hundred years that things had started to change. The technology and industry developed by the unTalented allowed them the tools to match, and in many cases exceed the feats once only accomplished by magic. Try as they might, the noble houses of the Talented couldn't stop progress.

Once the Council was formed things started to get better—at least for those at either end of the spectrum. The Council allowed the unTalented their technology and industry because they believed that without magic, they could never be a force to be reckoned with. By the time the Council realised how wrong they were, it was too late. The unTalented now owned their place in the world, for better or worse.

Unfortunately, half-bloods didn't get that same privilege. The little bit of magic we had made the unTalented think of us the same as they did our noble and often ruthless parents—with loathing and distrust. Yet we weren't accepted by the Talents, either. Though relations between the two groups had improved vastly over the years, half-bloods didn't fit into either; it was like being caught between a rock and a hard place. Come to think of it, it wasn't unheard of to have rocks thrown at us...

Harrod, of course, was raised within the cloistered confines of the Wall, amongst spoilt, egotist Talents who thought they had every right to rule the world. They were rich and powerful, they had magic that I could only dream of, they had a society in which every one of them was special. By using his Talent on me like that, he'd just confirmed that he didn't belong out here. He was one of *them*, and that would never change. In the short time I'd known him, I'd already come to think of him as a friend, but I wasn't so sure now. Maybe I couldn't trust him like I thought I could.

When the day finally came to an end, I was still sitting downstairs with a cold cup of tea, caught up in my own misery. Lenny had been hurt because of me. My home had been violated and I'd let myself become invested in a friendship that in all likelihood wouldn't work out. I liked Martin and I felt awful that I'd caused a rift between the two brothers, but I couldn't let go of who Harrod was, what he stood for. Heaving a sigh, I threw out my tea and headed upstairs.

Martin roused as I opened the door to my living space. He'd been sleeping on the couch and still looked bleary eyed. "You can keep snoozing, or I can make dinner," I said.

"Food," came the grunted reply.

I pulled open the pantry doors and peered in. Tired and miserable as I was, I didn't have the energy to cook something fancy. "I've got cheese, tomatoes, and a sandwich press. Will that do?"

Martin actually perked up a little at the suggestion. In about ten minutes' time, I had piping hot toasted sandwiches on the table. Was it only this morning we'd sat and had breakfast together? It felt like longer. Mentally groping around I searched for something to talk about, anything but the events from earlier today. I found nothing, so we ate in awkward silence.

"I'm sorry." His sudden words startled me.

"You? You didn't do anything." My voice was emphatic.

"I shouldn't have left Harrod alone to deal with the situation, not when there was a mess of people out there. I knew that."

"You're not his babysitter." I stood and started clearing the table, hoping to end the conversation.

Martin wasn't ready to let it drop. "What he did was wrong. He should never have threatened you. He never was good in a crisis; just falls back on the only thing he knew growing up. When a situation gets heated, shut it down. It's ingrained in him and sometimes it comes out, but he's a good person—the best I know. He's scared. The Lords are worried and things over the Wall are complicated right now. There's a chance things could get better but it's balancing on a knife's edge."

"I don't even know what that means. The nobles never leave the Inner City, they live in their own little fishbowl. What reason could they possibly have to change?"

There was a short silence while Martin tried to gather his thoughts.

"The Upper Houses and the unTalented leaders have been in negotiations. Our government – out here, I mean – want official recognition of their leadership. They want the Lords to put themselves under the rule of our laws when they're out here, and they want them monitored."

"I bet that went down like a ton of bricks," I muttered. I couldn't see any of the Houses agreeing to that.

To my surprise, Martin shook his head. "The Lords have divided into two factions. One half supports the proposal—well, in part—and the other reacted probably about as well as you'd expect. The faction that wins the election gets to decide. It really could mean big changes if the right group gets in."

"Right." I was unconvinced. "Where is Harrod, anyway?"

"Voting."

"It's tonight?" I hadn't realised it was so soon.

"Yeah."

"How does he think it'll go?"

Martin just shrugged, so I dropped it. Truthfully, I didn't see any hope that a progressive Council would ever rule inside the Inner City.

We didn't talk much after that—I was busy mulling over what he'd said about the Talents. I'd known about the three main factions battling for council positions—they basically boiled down to half-blood and unTalented supporters, half-blood and unTalented detractors, and the 'let's just kill everyone who's not us' group which was, thankfully, the smallest of the three.

There were more complexities, of course. Fae had recently been added to council sittings and there were various thoughts on the different classes of Otherworld denizens, but I was quite selfishly only interested in what it would mean for my own people. Shuddering at the prospect of a potentially bad outcome, I wondered how much it would change life outside the Wall.

Martin went back to sleep while I sat with coffee and bad TV. I wasn't tired. Lenny came up at some point and lay next to me, for which I was grateful. He was still exhausted but seemed otherwise fine. My poor boy. As he settled in, a flood of anger washed over me and then dissipated just as quickly, leaving me tired and numb. What could I do? It felt like I'd run out of options. So I sat, staring at silent infomercials until the sun rose.

Martin woke not long before sunrise and insisted I sleep. To pacify him, I went and lay down on my bed. I didn't think I'd sleep but I sank into a deep, disturbing dream that only ended when my door-bell rang, setting off an alert ward in my room. I stuck my head out the window—it was Harrod. I snatched up my wand to trace the spell that would un-ward the front door, then called to him that it was open. After he was inside I re-warded it.

A moment later, clomping footsteps sounded up the stairs to my flat. He came into the room and Martin looked at him expectantly. There was a moment of silence, then Harrod broke into a wide grin, arms spreading wide.

"We won, brother."

Martin let out a whoop and clapped his hands. The two embraced, slapping each other on the back.

"We... won?" I asked. "The sympathisers hold the majority?"

"Not just the majority." Harrod grabbed my arm in his excite-ment. "The High Seat. Abnett bloody won!"

I couldn't keep the shock from my face.

"How? There's no way a sympathiser could—"

"We've been working on this for years!" Harrod endured another back slap from Martin. "Since before I left the City. We thought we might have it, but it was close. The sympathisers run the Council fifteen to twelve. Not as big of a majority as we hoped, but having Abnett on the seat more than makes up for that. Some of the neutral families will start currying favour by leaning that way now that limp toad Morcolm is gone."

Morcolm was known for his refusal to take a side in the disagreements between Talented and not. Though he had half-bloods in his family and even a Fault—a second cousin or somewhat —he lacked the conviction to stand up to the dissenters on the Council.

"That's wonderful," I said, not as brightly as I could have. The feeling was there but I still felt sleep-muddled. I went into the kitchen, looking for coffee. It seemed Martin had already eaten.

"I made you breakfast; it's keeping warm in the oven," Martin said.

I opened it and took out a plate of food—beans, sausages, eggs, bread. It was warm and the eggs still soft, so I guessed it hadn't been there too long. I thanked him and sat down to eat as they continued talking.

Though I'd been told Harrod was an active part of a faction campaigning for equality across the three communities, I hadn't realised just how involved he was, or how much progress they had made. Though real acceptance might never happen, this might finally lead to a modicum of safety for the half-bloods.

Come to think of it, I knew of Abnett. He'd come into outer London every so often, meeting with the Talented out here and asking what they needed to continue their work, how the half-bloods needed help. There wasn't much that he could do, but it seemed like he cared. I'd never in a million years expected him to be elected to High Seat. It must have taken a really concerted effort and a lot of politicking to get him there. I wondered how secure his position was.

"What's Abnett like?" I asked. "I've only met him in passing."

The two men passed a look between them.

"He's... appreciative of the opportunity he's been given." Harrod's voice was guarded.

"He's a puppet." Martin was blunter in his appraisal. "But he's a puppet who knows what he is, and who put him in charge. He believes in the cause; he just doesn't have the leadership skills to run the council on his own."

"Why not find someone better then?"

Martin winced. "They were going to put Harrod's name forward until I came along. I sort of blew that opportunity for him."

Harrod snorted and I guessed he wasn't as enamoured with that idea as Martin had suggested. There was a lot I didn't know about this Talented outcast and his Fault of a brother. Martin offered to make tea and I nodded enthusiastically. He filled the kettle and held it out while Harrod absentmindedly heated it with a flick of his wand.

As Harrod traced his spell, he spoke. "That's not all the news I have. I spoke to a few people over there. It seems some of the community are aware of what's happening out here. Abnett got wind and was using it to boost his platform. In fact, there are a few rumours passing around about who's responsible."

My heart stopped. Finally, a lead, something we could act upon. "Who?"

"A man named Opius. He's from one of the oldest houses, but his line has more or less died out with him. Since losing his wife several years ago, he has gone into seclusion, only making a very occasional appearance."

"If he's disappeared, why is he a suspect?" Martin poured the tea.

"Because he is sick." Harrod gave me a knowing glance. "Very sick, if the stories are to be believed."

"The only illness a Talent healer can't cure..." I let the words trail off.

Harrod pointed a victorious finger at me. "Exactly. A magic-borne disease, one that saps Talent as well as physical strength."

"He has a motive, then," Martin said.

"More than that." Harrod took a sip of his tea. "I happened to bump into someone who saw him on her way to the Lords Conclave. She remarked at how hale he was, despite his condition. I believe the words she used were 'positively glowing', in fact."

"It's him," I said. "It must be him. But how do we *get* to him?"

It seemed Harrod even had an answer for that. "There's an event coming up that he's likely to put in an appearance at. A gala, one of the High Lords is hosting it to celebrate the new Council. I can get myself on the list, get a look at him. Maybe even corner him, if we play our cards right. If I can goad him into attacking me, it'd pull the whole City down on his head."

"You can't do that," I said, almost choking on a mouthful of food. "It's not safe. We don't know how he's doing this or how strong he is."

"Actually, I think I do." Harrod paused, collecting his thoughts. "Know how he's doing it, that is. I managed to find out some information about the weapon he's using... Seems one of the grails has gone missing. The Guardians haven't confirmed it, but the rumour is spreading and they haven't put a stop to it." He spread his hands in a wide shrug. "It makes perfect sense."

Grails were old, dark magic used back in the days when offspring like me were sacrificed. The blood rite would pass the power of the victim to the one leading the ceremony. The exact details of how were unknown, but this seemed to confirm the theory we'd been working on. If this Opius had gotten his hands on one of these, he'd have had to make it past the Guardians, or made a deal with one of them. That alone made him a very dangerous man—one with either an awful lot of power or one who had nothing to lose. The second scared me more.

"Harrod, you're seriously considering going against someone armed with a *grail*? You don't even know how it works, how to fight against it. That it came from the Guardians makes it even more dangerous."

"You're right of course. I'll need to talk to them. They're the only ones who know how they work, perhaps they'll tell me how to stop it. Then we can—

"What?" I interjected. "Talk with who? You can't seriously intend to seek out the *Guardians*?" It was too dangerous. Hey, I might not like the guy but that didn't mean I wanted him spit roasted and fed to a horde of hungry pixies.

"I don't have a choice, they're the only ones who might know how to stop it," he replied calmly.

"There has to be another way. I can send Gibble instead."

"They won't give a boggart the time of day," Harrod said. "It has to be a human. My status as a Talent will help—it would be a risk for them to attack me without provocation; they wouldn't give up their council seats over a bit of sport."

He had a point, but dammit, I couldn't let him do this. Not for me. Not after what I'd said about him. There was only one thing to do.

"I'm coming too." I waved my fork at Harrod, cutting off his protest. "Don't even bother to argue. These are *my* people at risk and it's *my* life on the line. I have to be there."

"That's settled then," Martin said. "Shall I pack sandwiches for the three of us?"

Chapter Sixteen

After doing our best to convince Martin to stay behind, we finally relented when he threatened to follow us on his own. That would have been a suicide mission. It was going to be hard enough to keep him alive travelling with us, but for a mortal man to walk through the Otherworld alone was a guaranteed death sentence —a long, painful one.

It wasn't a trip we could make without preparation. We would be on high alert for the trip and there was no guessing how long it would take. Harrod wanted to reach out to some contacts to smooth our journey, and Martin and I both needed rest. I'd have to find someone to look after Lenny, too—normally Gibble would do that, but I didn't want him left alone at night after what happened.

After some discussion, we agreed to meet again in three days. Meanwhile, Harrod promised to have someone watch over me at all times. I chafed a little at that but didn't argue. My safety was more important than my pride.

When Gibble arrived later in the day to help finish the cleaning and restocking, I almost told him of our journey. He might know a safe way through to the Guardians, or he might know someone who could help us on the other side. I opened my mouth to ask, then changed my mind. The mostly likely answer he would give me was "Don't."

"I'm not opening the shop on Wednesday. I'm spending the day with Martin and Harrod. You don't need to come in." He just shrugged, not giving any indication of whether he'd show up anyway. He probably would—I'd have to make sure I left early to avoid him.

Guilt nagged at me after I said it. Gibble had looked after me to some degree or another all my life. Now, however, that protective streak could very well cause him to try and stop me. I busied myself putting away the stock I'd finished last night, trying to avoid looking at my ancient friend or thinking about my upcoming journey. The situation we were walking into would be dangerous. We would have to be prepared, but I didn't want to dwell on it more than I needed to in case I lost my nerve completely.

Most of my day was spent fidgeting, pacing and fiddling with stock, trying to dodge Gibble as much as I could. I was relieved when I received a visit from DCI Greyson late that afternoon. He arrived as I was closing the shop, his suit wrinkled and hair sticking out at odd angles. *Someone's had a rough day.* I eagerly took the opportunity to shoo Gibble off while I spoke to him.

We exchanged pleasantries, then stood around awkwardly for a moment. I wasn't sure how to ask about the file that had been dropped at my door, in case it hadn't been him.

"Hey, I just wanted to come by and check that everything is ok. I heard there was a disturbance here yesterday?"

You know how in movies the girl is all strong and independent and doesn't tell anyone what's happening in case they get hurt? I get that impulse. I also watch a lot of movies and know it never goes well.

"I was robbed and I think it was the killer. He's come for me more than once now. This time, he hurt my dog—and he took back the murder weapon."

"The weapon—you mean you had it? You didn't tell anyone?" Greyson shook his head in irritation. "What the *hell* were you thinking? We've been searching for this guy for months without a damn thing to go on, while you've got the goddamn murder weapon and didn't tell the police."

I shrank back at his anger. I hadn't even thought of it that way.

"Look, I did try to call you. They said..." I trailed off.

"They told you the morons at the O.C.U. have the case, didn't they?" He sighed. "So you thought there was no point, that it wouldn't make a difference. That the police wouldn't care because you're a half-blood."

I shrugged. He'd said what I was trying not to. Looking away, he ran his fingers through his hair in frustration.

"I know the O.C.U. has a bad rep. They're poorly managed and full of idiots, but that doesn't mean the rest of us aren't trying. I'm an officer of the law, I'm not just going to let some psychopath run around killing people. If you have something, share it with me. I know I can't promise much but I will do what I can."

"Ok." I could agree to that. "But if you're not with the Other-world Crime Unit, why are you even on the case?"

"I caught the first death before we realised Talents were involved. The unit muscled in but made a botch of it and didn't care. When this latest one fell in my lap—your friend, Keely—I refused to make that same mistake again. I refused to let the case drop, so technically, it's being run by two departments."

"That was brave. I don't imagine your superiors were pleased." My respect for the man was growing. It was unusual for a mortal to care so much about what happened to a half-blood.

"I'll face the ramifications later. For now, I've been allowed to work alongside O.C.U. and I'd like to get it solved before anyone else dies. Can I rely on your help?" His eyes searched my face, looking for a sign that he could trust me.

I told him everything that had already happened, everything I knew. He took notes and as I described the attacks, he seemed to show genuine concern for my safety. Still, I didn't mention our plans

—I couldn't be sure he wouldn't try to interfere. When I finished, he offered me a protective detail.

"No, that's fine. I have friends watching over me; Talents. I have Gibble, too—yeah, he's my shop assistant."

"I still think it would be better if my team—"

I raised a hand to cut him off. "Look, I really mean this in the nicest way possible, but... this guy is a full Talent. He's powerful, maybe more than we know, and he has connections to the Houses. I don't want your people getting hurt. Even if he comes after me again —which he might not, now he has his knife back—I really don't think your people could stop him."

Greyson shifted uncomfortably, but he knew I was right. They wouldn't let anyone with magic on the force and without it, they didn't stand a chance against a man like Opius. He sighed again and said farewell, reminding to me to take care and call him if anything else came up. I promised him I would, and I almost meant it.

When Gibble arrived the next morning, he came straight up to my rooms to seek me out.

"You not be doing this thing. You must promise me you will not."

"What thing?" I asked innocently.

"I know you did hear that rumour. I know it did be passed to Talent-friend. And I know *you* be stupid, so I think me, 'she be going to the Others, Gibble'. I be right?" Gibble folded his arms across his chest, waiting.

"I'm *stupid*?" I exclaimed.

"You be going?"

"Well... yes, but—"

Gibble threw his hands up, almost hitting the pendant light above. "Then you be stupid. Stupid humans, thinking you be going to have tea with those who be killing you. You not be going."

"Gibble, you can't keep me here." Gibble's wrinkled, hairless brows pulled in and his mouth puckered. The look on his face broke my heart. The crazy old boggart was actually, genuinely worried about me. That guilty feeling kicked in again. "Gib, I'll be fine. We're going together, me, Harrod and Martin. We'll take runes, we'll follow the rules and we'll be very, very careful. I'll come back to you, I promise."

"Gibble knew you be stupid." He dropped the mournful expression and cracked a wrinkly grin. "So, Gibble decide to be stupid with. Gibble coming too."

Cripes. This was going to be one hell of an adventure...

Time flew by, as it does when you want it to crawl, and the day I dreaded came quickly. There was only one port-gate outside of the city that led to the Otherworld. It was nearer to Martin and Harrod's home than mine so we decided to meet there first and all leave together.

The house—manor, really—was in the richer part of London and butted up against the Wall, as some of the most affluent houses did. To say the house was large was an understatement. It was a tiny freaking castle. As we approached the gates they opened themselves, creaking loudly.

We made our way up the driveway to a large, wooden front door framed by pillars topped by... gargoyles. The man had gargoyles at his door. What next, the front door was going to open ominously by itself like a B-grade horror movie? I raised my hand to the knocker... the door opened ominously by itself and I stifled a nervous giggle. Gibble looked at me, the niceties of humour apparently passing over him.

We went inside and found Martin waiting. He shushed me. "Don't laugh. He thinks it's actually scary. If he finds out how bad it is, he'll get rid of the only source of amusement in my life."

I laughed again, and a little knot of tension unwound. I was terrified, but I could still laugh. That was a good thing.

Martin looked over my shoulder. "Gibble's coming too? Who will look after Lenny? We don't know how long we'll be gone."

"Melanie said she'd—

"Is ok." Gibble spoke at that same time as me and I stopped, surprised. "Gibble have friend watching house. He be feeding Lenny-dog if we not be returning."

"Wait—what? You have someone watching my house? Since when?"

The boggarts massive shoulders rose in a slow shrug. "Since it be looking like you be in danger. Gibble not be there all the times. Barg be watching. Barg owe Gibble many favours. Barg *very* bad at gambling. Gibble earn more favours from him easy." His chest swelled with pride at that last part.

"Melanie's going over to check on Lenny. He won't eat her or anything will he?"

Gibble paused. "No, no... well, I think he would not."

Martin led the way into the villainous lair—this place was too over the top to ever be called an actual house—to find Harrod putting the finishing touches on a rune of protection. He greeted us distractedly, before speaking, "Did you find the place all right?"

"Yes," I said without a trace of a smile.

"It look like the house of the Family Addams," Gibble said in his serious baritone. It was too much, Martin and I nearly choked trying to hold back our laughter.

Harrod looked at him. "What? What do you mean?"

"Mortals have pictures on boxes. Call it tell-ee." Gibble explained. I refused to look at Martin lest I burst into giggles.

Harrod opened his mouth as if to ask what he was talking about, then shook his head and turned to us. "It's ready when we are," he said.

Four adventurers, heading off to certain death. Well, hopefully not certain but there was a fair chance of it. Harrod and Martin both carried knapsacks and when I opened one that Harrod passed to me, I found an assortment of wards, charms and...

"Sandwiches? Martin, this isn't a goddamn picnic. If we stop for lunch, it's *us* that'll be eaten." I wasn't sure what he expected this trip to be like, but really, sandwiches?

"It can't hurt to have them." He shrugged nonchalantly. "We can eat them on our way home."

I sighed. *Humans.* No wonder Gibble had such a poor opinion of us.

Though none of us wanted to leave the safe confines of the city, we knew there was no point delaying. We set off, Harrod warding the gargantuan door behind us.

It only took a few minutes to walk to the circle of gates. Being so close to a major thoroughfare like this was a reminder of the money Harrod had behind him—real estate here didn't come cheap.

We donned the runes, worked onto leather straps that hung around our necks. They would help ward off some of the more unsavoury creatures of the Otherworld. Gibble didn't need them— as long as he didn't piss anyone off directly, he was pretty safe in the Otherworld. There was a moment of awkward shuffling while we sorted out the contact points—we all had to be touching each other as we went through to make certain we landed in the same place. Martin and I both clasped one of Harrod's hands. My other hand was in Gibble's—not needed, because he could control his landing, but much welcomed. Harrod uttered the words that turned on the port-gate and we stepped into it. Everything turned inside out.

My breath was sucked from my body and my eyes felt like they were being pushed out of my head. I was weightless. I weighed more than concrete. I was full of fire and ice, I was liquid like water and solid like stone.

I fell.

The ground met my body with a jarring thud. Carefully, I picked myself up from the ground amidst the grunt of my companions, not letting go of Harrod's hand just yet.

"Everyone here?" I asked.

"I am here, you are here, clever man is here and little man with little head is here." Gibble's voice rumbled next to me.

"I think he means you." Martin's voice came out of the darkness. "I know I'm the clever one."

"I don't have a little head," Harrod complained. "First my house, now my head. You need better servants."

"I not be servant," Gibble exclaimed at the same I said, "He's *not* my servant."

"All right, all right. You can let go now, I think it's safe."

Harrod's hand left mine and I stood carefully, pulling out my wand, trying to be ready for what was to come.

Chapter Seventeen

I traced a spell, throwing a ball of light into the air. It lit the area we were in wanly, casting eerie shadows around us. A moment later, Harrod threw up one of his own—his was brighter and the light it created spread far into the distance like a tiny sun. I dismissed mine, embarrassed at its dim light.

"Save your strength," Harrod said, seemingly unaware of how condescending it sounded.

Our faces were pale in the blue light. Despite its brightness, shadows wound around us, moving in a way they really shouldn't have been. Around my neck, the rune I wore felt heavy, like it had an added weight in this strange world.

"Remember, don't stray off the path, don't talk to anyone, don't touch anything," Harrod said.

"This be Gibble's home. Gibble knows rules, silly mortal."

The ground was uneven and I slipped my hand into Gibble's as I spoke to help my balance. "I don't think he was talking to you, Gib."

He looked down at me briefly and smiled before shooting a glance back at Harrod. "Oh. Apologies, silly mortal."

"Hold hands," I said. "If we form a chain, it'll be harder to get... lost." I didn't want to say taken. I didn't even want to think it.

I was still holding Gibble's hand and I reached for Harrod. He took my hand. "Martin?" he said.

"Yes, that's me holding yours."

Harrod went white. "Nobody move."

"What's wrong?" I asked as he looked towards Martin, terrified.

"No one is holding my other hand," he whispered.

Martin looked down in confusion. Harrod and Gibble both reached out to grab Martin, just as he was yanked away, then dematerialised in a puff of darkness. Harrod tried to let go of my hand, to go after him but I held on. Gibble grabbed him by the scruff and hauled him back.

"Martin!" Harrod screamed after his brother. "Martin!"

I pulled him around, yanking at his arm to get him to face me. "We'll find him; we'll get him back!" I said.

Harrod's breath heaved and he trembled with the effort of staying put. He looked out into the Otherworld, sending his light globe in the direction we'd last seen Martin. It revealed nothing but an empty field covered in purple grass.

"What you bring for offerings?" Gibble asked.

"Offerings?" Harrod panted, eyes darting around, still looking for a face in the darkness.

"Yes, you want see Guardians, you must bring offering. You no bring offering?"

"No," Harrod said.

"Oh. Is ok then. Your friend be with Guardians. They think him offering!"

"Oh, Gods." If Harrod's face was pale before it was positively white now. "What will they do to him?"

"Oh, they might play with him a little but they not hurt him until you there."

"And when we're there?" I asked, worried

"Well... we must be telling them the playing is the offering, not the human's own self. They will not be very happy and you might have to fight to get him back, but maybe they just give him." Gibble shrugged. "Depends if he good at playing."

"Playing... what?" I wasn't sure if I actually wanted to hear the answer.

"Oh. Well. They not be hurting him." Was it possible for a boggart to blush?

Right. Definitely didn't want the answer then. If the Guardians were Fae, I could imagine what 'play' meant. Martin might actually enjoy it, as long as Harrod didn't get us all killed when we got there. Judging by the look on his face, he knew what 'play' meant too. I mentally reduced our chances of survival from even odds down to about four percent.

We set off along a glittering path, the three of us holding hands awkwardly. The small noises we made were swallowed by the deafening silence. Though it seemed we were walking on a path through an open field of green flowers, the night pressed down on us like we were trapped in a closed corridor with stale air and no space to breathe. I dropped my eyes so I could only see the path and focused on the two hands I was holding.

Gibble's hand was rough and inhuman. As a child, that hand had pulled me to safety more than once. Falling out of trees, off walls, once out of a window while trying to charm a bird the way they did in movies. Though slow and lumbering in his everyday movement, Gibble could move like lightning when compelled.

In my other hand, Harrod's felt warm and... human. I thought about my anger towards him and realised it had been slowly dissipating. His reaction to the way Martin was taken had exhausted it. The guilt and fear in Harrod's eyes burned into my memory, and I knew I would never forget it. Despite our differences, my heart ached for him. The brothers were close and relied on each other so much. I cared about Martin of course and wanted him back, but not like Harrod did.

We travelled in silence, walking quickly. I sensed Harrod's desire to hurry, felt it myself, but I knew running was pointless. The Otherworld wasn't a place of distances—it was said you would get to your destination when you were wanted, not a moment before. God help you if no one wanted to see you. Stories of Talented seeking audience here and never returning were common, though most did make it out eventually.

Suddenly, a light appeared ahead of us. Gibble rumbled a noise—not worry, but not exactly happy either.

"What is it?" I asked.

"Not where we wants to be," was his grumbled reply.

Harrod stopped at that.

"You can't turn around. They'll take us where they want us to go, nowhere else, you *know* that. Even if you tried to go back to look for him, you'd just end up somewhere else entirely Harrod," I said.

He did know, better than I did. Harrod pressed his lips together, set his shoulders and continued walking along the narrow path.

We pressed on, the light coming towards us forming into the glow of a gathering. It looked like some kind of night market. Shanty stalls lined the sides of the path, which wound between stalls but never crossed over itself. Some of the vendors were creatures I had never seen. Others I knew, or at least knew of. We passed a goblin hawking charms for those crossing the Otherworld. On our other side a giant, gnarled and wrinkled, yelled at another one in what sounded like the old tongue. Up ahead, just off the path, an old Fae crone sat on a stool with an empty blanket in front of her. She had white hair to her feet and blank eyes that stared at nothing. Still, I couldn't help the feeling she was watching me, and my eyes followed her as we passed. Next to her, a creature made of tree bark and winding vines swayed in the absent breeze.

As we walked the space became more crowded, though no one crossed our path. We gripped hands tightly, and I for one wasn't ashamed to admit it was partly out of fear. Harrod kept his head down and would flinch if one of the creatures started towards us, though Gibble seemed his usual, easy self.

At first, the creatures ignored us, going about their business. As our winding, silver path drew us deeper into the market, eyes of purple and shining silver turned to follow us. Soon, they were calling us, begging us to try their wares, have a bite, a sip, a feel of some fabric. They clustered around the edge of the track, following us as we tried to ignore them. Still, none of them stepped onto the path itself. They were holding back, or something was holding them back; I wasn't sure how long that would last.

As I watched them more closely, I realised they seemed afraid of Gibble. As his big head swung from side to side, those caught by his stern eyes shrank back a little. He seemed to be able to sense when they were just a little too close and would turn that way in time to make them retreat.

Just as I thought we'd make it through without incident, a small, knobbled man standing close to the road thrust his hands out and grabbed my skirt. I screamed, and Gibble let go of my hand. He swung his arm, knocking the small creature back like a toy. It was suddenly surrounded by others of its kind. The cluster of snarling Otherworlders swarmed over each other, all glaring at Gibble and hissing through sharp teeth. They advanced.

I looked in horror as Gibble swelled to twice his normal size. As he grew, sharp horns sprouted from his skin along his arms. Hands, once like mine if a little large and rough, stretched and distorted so that they looked like claws. His mouth opened and sharp teeth jutted from his jaw. He roared into the darkness "These humans be MINE!!"

The creatures scrambled back, fleeing into the night. Gibble swung around, screaming the words again to direct his challenge at all who watched. "THESE HUMANS BE MINE!"

Then, he faced us, fury and hunger on his horrifying face fading into a look of calm certainty, as he spoke the words one more time in a low and menacing growl. "These humans be *mine*."

As the words left his mouth the third time, the night market vanished into nothingness. The sudden darkness was punctured only by a ball of Talent-light.

I stared at Gibble, who was now cloaked in shadow despite the light from Harrod's globe. *My Gibble.* My Gibble, with horns on his arms and fury in his eyes. As I watched, he deflated somewhat. He did not change back, though.

In a voice closer to what he normally used, Gibble said "You, all of you, be bound to me. You be under my protection, and that be no small thing. There be a price... but now, I must be going. This place has taken a thing from me, a thing that makes me... like you. Like humans. It be taking some time to find it again. Go now, be safe. I be returning when I be my own self again."

With that, he touched his clawed hand to my face. So gentle, this terrifying beast. As he loped off into the darkness, I felt tears well in my eyes. I prayed I would see him again.

Harrod turned to go but I resisted, just for a moment. He looked back at me.

"I know you care about him. We can't stop moving, though." He pulled gently at my hand.

"I can't just leave him behind. He's my friend." I jerked my hand back, letting go of Harrod.

"You don't have a choice." His voice was hard and it pierced the night, sounding loud in the silence.

"How can you not care? He came with us to keep us safe, to keep *me* safe. I'm not like you, remember? I'm weak, I'm the bottom of the shit pile when it comes to power. He came to protect me, like he's always done."

"Of course I bloody care!" Harrod's fists clenched and he flushed red with anger. "I care about Gibble, but he can look after himself. Martin can't. He has no power, nothing. I'm the one who dragged him into this and I'm the one who brought him on this fool's errand. You say you're weak? He doesn't have a damn trick to keep him alive down here. I knew that, and I still let him come. We *have* to go to him before they tear him apart."

I knew he was right, but part of me still wanted to be angry. We were moving towards his friend, but away from mine. I think he could see that on my face because he looked down. His shoulders slumped and his voice lowered.

"Look, I know you... I'm..." He sucked in a breath, held it for a moment,then blew it out slowly. "Gods, I don't blame you for hating me because of what I am and I know I've done some terrible things, but I'm *trying*, Emma. I'm trying my absolute damnedest for people like you, and people like Martin. I don't want to be the person I was before, but I'm still trying to figure out what to be instead. Trying to do that while I keep everyone alive is *really bloody hard!*"

I was completely taken aback. I started walking, unsure of what to say. A tug at my hand pulled me back again.

"I'm sorry." He spoke the words so softly I almost missed them.

"Why? This isn't your fault. Everything you said was right, we need to keep moving." My voice wasn't as steady as I'd hoped it would be.

"No, I mean I'm sorry for hurting you when... I shouldn't have reacted that way."

"I... yeah, you're right. You shouldn't have." Mustering up a tiny smile, I slid my hand further into his. "Still, if you hadn't, that guy would be crispy fries right now."

"You could do that?"

I laughed softly. "No, not by a long shot. I wanted to, though."

Silence again as we walked side by side, still gripping hands. The path we walked had no landmarks, no signposts, nothing to even show we were making progress.

I took a breath, let it out, and spoke. "I'm sorry too. I let my own issues get in the way from the beginning and that was really unfair of me. You've done nothing but help, and you didn't even have to do that. I know not all Talented are monsters—my dad, he was amazing and he loved me just the same as his other children. I just got so used to the rest of you—*them*, being really awful."

He sighed. "I don't even know where I fit anymore. I'm not one of them... but in a way, I still am."

"I guess... you belong with us."

He swallowed, opened his mouth and almost spoke. Then, his eyes widened at something off in the distance. "Look, over there. Can you see it?"

I could. It was a slit of light, off to the side. I looked down and sure enough, our path turned in that direction. We'd been standing still so whatever it was, was moving toward us. That's how things worked down here, though, so we increased our pace, hurrying along the road that now led us straight into the light.

We didn't run, that was too dangerous, but we moved as fast as we could. It seemed the Guardians were ready to see us, for the light moved towards us faster than our steps would have allowed. Before long we stood before an old stone arch, filled with glowing light. The glittering path we walked went right up to it. Gripping Harrod's hand tightly and taking a deep breath I took one last step and entered, my friend beside me.

We emerged into a cavernous room. White walls reached high over our heads to a domed ceiling that supported the biggest chandelier I had ever seen. A handful of people clustered around the edges of the room, all of them more Fae than any Fae I'd seen. Tall, slender bodies, bright, cat-slit eyes, red lips, and those who smiled at our entry showed pointed teeth. Oh, they were beautiful, but very, very dangerous.

One particular pair of eyes caught mine. A corner of her rosebud mouth turned up as she saw me watching her. She approached, the white coils of hair perched elegantly on top of her head swaying as she walked. Her bright diamond jewellery glittered under the chandelier, but that wasn't what had caught my eye. Something about the line of her jaw, the brilliance of her hair. *And those eyes...* I started when I recognised her as the dirty crone from the markets, and again when I recognised the meaning of the power that saturated her. *Guardian.*

"You seek aid?" she asked in a slow drawl.

"Yes, great lady." Harrod offered a deep and respectful bow. He let go of my hand to do so and I suddenly felt less sure of myself.

"Why should we provide it?" another of the Guardians asked. He was fine boned with hair just a little redder than was natural and a smattering of perfectly placed freckles. His cherry lips should have clashed with his hair but somehow, he just looked... perfect.

"We seek to return an item that has been taken from you." Harrod now bowed at the second speaker.

"Oh, child," came the voice of a young girl. "So much formality. You Lordlings, always so stuffy. We shall retire to the parlour and speak like friends." I turned to find a human girl of about nine years old standing behind us. She had dark, perfectly curled hair framing porcelain skin and a dress in the style of a Victorian-era princess. Despite her young age and human appearance, her presence was every bit as commanding as her fellow Guardians.

She waved her hand. The cluster of Fae disappeared and the room swirled. A feeling of fatigue washed over me but I fought it, staying awake by force of will alone. My stomach lurched and then everything settled. We were now standing in... well, a parlour. It looked like something out of a Victorian manse, with lavish drapes and intricately carved furniture.

Three Guardians, the crone, the man and another, sat around a table and played with dice, their tones muted and their words indistinguishable.

The tiny Guardian that had created the room waved me to sit as she herself climbed into an oversized chair. I perched on a love seat in which a sleeping Harrod reclined.

"Is he going to be..." I swallowed.

"Oh, he'll be perfectly fine." The child-Guardian giggled. "I thought it would be nice to converse for a moment without all the bowing and apple-polishing."

I wasn't particularly reassured by her words, as stories about those who put a foot wrong with the Fae didn't tend to end well. These? They weren't just any Fae, these were the Lords and Ladies, they ruled supreme with powers that no human could dream of wielding. I wondered again at her human appearance. A disguise, perhaps?

"Now, tell me what you came for my dear." Her tinkling voice soothed my anxiety. I knew it to be false, an enchantment woven to lull me into false security.

"We came for your assistance, great one." I inclined my head respectfully but kept my eyes on her.

"Oh please, don't tell me you're as bad as that one." She waved a hand delicately at Harrod.

"Very well. We came to ask for help. We think a Talent Lord stole from you and is using the thing he took to hurt my people."

"And your people are?"

"Half-bloods. Those with Talent and unTalented blood combined."

Despite her youthful appearance, the Guardian raised a delicate eyebrow with all the grace of a well-practised aristocrat. "Why do the Talents not protect you from this threat if he is one of theirs?"

I had to step carefully here. Every question would have a purpose and often not the one apparent.

"The Talent Lords do not believe him to be a threat to them." That was the prudent answer. I pressed my lips together to stop myself from saying something scathing about their motivation.

"And yet he is a threat to their children. Do they not care?" The child-Guardian looked at me with wide, innocent eyes. It was easy to believe she asked genuinely, except that she was one of *them*. She knew exactly why those bastards hid behind their Wall and refused to help. Still, it wouldn't be wise to speak the truth. Not here.

"I can't speak to their motivations. However, if I—if my friends and I can stop him, we'll return the item he's using to you." My heart ached to pour out my frustration at the Talent Lords, and it was a real effort to hold back. I ground my teeth until they hurt. There was magic here, something compelling me to say more than I wanted to. After a moment, it passed.

"We do not wish to have it back. It was not stolen, but given freely." The Guardian's voice lost its musical quality and was now flat and serious.

Uh oh. Given freely? One of the Fae—one of the Guardians themselves—had *given* Opius a grail? That was bad news.

"Ah." I reached over to give Harrod a surreptitious pinch on the leg, but he didn't rouse from his sleep. "Well then, I think my friends and I should depart then. It seems we misunderstood the situation and are wasting your time. You have my deepest apologies."

The Lady leaned forward and poured tea. She held a cup out which I took, but didn't drink from.

"You have nothing to fear from us, my love." The child-Guardian caressed my hand. "Our intent was not for harm to come to you, then or now. Eat, drink, indulge in our world. It does not suit us to keep you here. Not this time. Now, tell me why you think you need to take on this threat alone?"

"Alone? No, I..." I realised it was true. Despite Harrod accompanying me here and all the offers of help he and others had given, in my mind, I intended to set out on this mission alone. "I don't want my friends at risk."

"And yet you are willing to risk a friend of theirs?" The Guardian shook her head. "You are the ward of an ancient creature who's bond to you will be severed if you die. It will take from him much of the sentience he has earned over time. You are the linchpin of a community that is fractured. If you leave them, they will scatter. You are the light that will guide one friend to do great things. If you extinguish it, he shall fail. You are the stone that another will lean upon when things are darkest. If you crumble, so shall he. You are the key to their success. You are... so much more than you realise, Emmeline."

"My name is Emma." My mouth was dry and my stomach roiled at hearing the name I once used.

"And yet, you are also Emmeline. You may have discarded it but it is still yours. You will one day claim it again." The child-Guardian lifted her head, considering me. "For now, though, you may pretend."

I looked at her, unsure of what to make of all she said. She turned to Harrod and handed him a cup. Just like that, he sat up, lucid and apparently unaware that he'd been sleeping.

"Ah, thank you, great lady."

The great lady rolled her eyes.

"Might we petition your Ladyship for assistance in our quest? We would be most humbly grateful."

"You do not need it." She sighed as if bored and kicked her feet, swishing her full skirt. "The way to defeat the dream stalker resides in the one he seeks the most. You shall prevail and you do not require our help to do so. Now hurry along back to your little world. I grow bored with your presence."

"Ah. Well then. Thank you, esteemed Guardian," Harrod bowed his head and I mimicked him, trying to look like a good, deferent little human.

Harrod paused, took a breath, and spoke again. "When we arrived here, we provided a sampling of... ahhh... a mortal. I hope you've had sufficient time to enjoy him. As we have the answer we came for, it is now time for us to collect our offering and depart your realm." Harrod's voice was clear with only the slightest tremor to indicate his anxiety. We should have talked about this, rehearsed it instead of having our petty argument.

The Guardian snapped her fingers and Martin was led in by two Fae. I say led because he looked like he couldn't find his way out of a paper bag. His eyes were drowsy and lovesick and his shirt was gone.

Apart from some red scratches on his torso and a dozen love bites across his neck and shoulder, he didn't seem to be injured.

"You want it back?" one of the Fae said. I guessed he was male. He laughed, baring sharply pointed teeth. "You are fortunate I did not have the time to partake in this gift myself then. He may not have been returned in such good condition."

"I'm quite inclined to keep him actually," said the other. "Do you truly wish him to return with you?"

"Yes," Harrod and I spoke the word at the same time.

"Well then, if you want him you may have him. If you can't keep him, however, we shall."

Martin was thrust at us. Harrod caught him as the one who'd spoken snapped her fingers, causing Martin to slump to the floor unconscious.

"Hold on," Harrod said, gripping Martin's arm. "It's a test. For the sake of the Gods, hold on and don't let go, or we'll lose him forever!"

As I reached for Martin's other arm, I shot a beseeching look at the Parlour Guardian—probably not her title but I didn't know what that was. She just watched serenely. I guessed the platitudes she'd extended to me hadn't covered Martin as well. I grabbed Martin's arm as instructed, just as it changed. Human skin transformed into rough scales, moving under my hand.

I'd heard of this test; it was one of their favourites. As long as we won, as long as we didn't let go, any hurt done to us would be an illusion and Martin truly would be returned to us safely and unharmed. If we let go, however, the damage caused would be real... and there *would* be damage.

Using both hands to ensure a steady grip, I didn't flinch as the hand I held became that of a beast, scaled like a fish and gnarled with long, silver talons. I dared not look at his face, for I knew that it was likely to be the face of some creature used to scare children into behaving. It flexed, and claws dug into the flesh of my arm. I weathered the pain, knowing worse was to come.

The claw shifted and writhed as it transformed into rough tree bark. I was holding a branch and green vines snaked over my wrist. Branches sprouted from the limb I gripped. One punctured my hand and I let out a scream. I cut off the sound, forcing my mind to hold onto the knowledge that it wasn't real, it was just an illusion. I closed my eyes and concentrated, blocking out the pain and sensations, focusing on the soft, human flesh I knew I held. As I did so, the pain vanished and I held Martin's arm again as it should be.

"It's not real," I said. "Dammit Harrod, it's *not real*."

I risked a glance at Harrod who still yelled in agony. His hands were punctured and bleeding. If he let go, our only chance at getting Martin home was me. I knew I couldn't outdo a Talent in a Fae test. Harrod was a thousand times stronger than me, so if he failed...

I had no further time for thought as Martin's arm burst into flame. White hot fire licked at my arms and I wept. *Not real, not real.* I reminded myself, trying to block out Harrod's screams and the scent of burning flesh. Again, the pain subsided and the wounds healed. Harrod's screams had turned into broken whimpering. *Why isn't he healing between transformations?* Gods, I hoped this would end soon. I didn't know how much more either of us could endure.

Writhing. Another change. This time, Martin's limb became slippery and long, growing out into a giant tentacle. I made the mistake of looking at him and came face to face with a beast from hell.

Red eyes glowed from sunken sockets. His mouth was open and filled with razor-sharp teeth, dripping venomous liquid. It dribbled on to my arm and seared like the flames had. The giant tentacle I gripped continued to grow, elongating and slithering up my arm, to wrap around my neck. *No. No, no, NO!* It wrapped around my throat and started to squeeze. *Not real.* I rolled my eyes to Harrod, who had fallen on the floor, holding out an arm charred into blackness. *He let go.*

The monster tightened its grip on my neck and I felt my airways crush. Pressure built behind my eyes and my vision went blurry. *Not real.* My heart pounded, seeking oxygen that wasn't there as another tentacle wrapped around my chest, forcing out the last remnant of air. *Not real.* My hand went numb and started to slip. *Not... real...*

I couldn't do it. Couldn't pass the test, couldn't save my friend. I was weak and useless like I'd always been. How dare I think I could pass this test, or that I could take on a powerfully Talented killer by myself?

My mind flashed to the friends I'd lost, then ran past the ones I still had—friends still at risk from a man who traded innocent lives for power. A white hot rage filled me. *No.* No, I was NOT going to lose this battle. Somehow, despite the crushing pressure on my throat and chest, I heaved a breath and let out a scream of pure anger.

Anger not just at the Fae for trying to take away my friend. Anger, not just at the killer who wanted my life. Pure, unfettered rage. Rage at my siblings for bullying me, at the Talents for ostracising me, at the mortals for fearing me. Rage at my own inadequacies, at my misjudgement of Harrod, at the harm to my dog, at the threat to my Gibble. All of it rushed out in a thunderous scream.

The beast disappeared and the pressure around my throat vanished. Martin stood before me, a wavering form. He dissolved into a liquid puddle on the floor but his arm where I gripped it stayed warm and solid. It was like a dream; two things that shouldn't have been able to exist together, did.

I reached out and took Harrod's blackened arm too. As I touched it, the charred skin fell away and was whole underneath. I held them both as Martin shifted again, into soft sand, trickling through cracks in the floor. Still, his arm was solid. The final change, this one unexpected. A man, but not Martin. I knew him—it was a Talent, one I knew. It was Jacoby Priest, the man who'd stopped a fight in my shop. Confusion melted into pure relief as Martin became Martin again, whole and unscathed. I let out a sob and pulled him close.

"You now have two things you will need to win the battle ahead." The Crone spoke. She and her companions had left their game of dice to watch us. "Take care, dear one, and save yourself for the bigger fight ahead." The Crone regarded us with sombre eyes, but the child ran up and embraced me, smiling with glee. She let go, then waved at me.

With a whoosh and a pop, we were sucked back into the void between worlds and unceremoniously dumped on the other side.

Chapter Eighteen

I opened my eyes to the smell of fresh grass. An ancient oleander tree towered over us, bright sunlight prickling at my eyes through the branches I stared up at. Turning my head, I saw a neatly clipped hedge.

"Martin?" I called, my voice tremulous. "Harrod?"

"Mmrph." As incomprehensible grunts go, this one sounded classier than most. Harrod, I guessed.

"Martin?" I lifted my head to look for him, worry spiking until I saw him lying on the ground, staring at me with a goofy smile on his face.

"Mmmm. Mmff." Ok, he was vocal. Sort of. I rolled onto my stomach and pushed up onto my arms.

I wondered aloud where we were; Harrod told me we were back at his house. A quick look around to check for topiaries in the shape of dragons, or an endless maze found only a simple patio, the tree above me and a box hedge border. It seemed Harrod's landscaper had more taste than his decorator. We shook ourselves off and headed inside. Harrod made tea while I sat with Martin, warily eyeing him from across the room. It was disconcerting, to say the least. The Fae-spell lingered, leaving him with a heady grin and sleepy eyes. Harrod came back and after some food and drink, Martin seemed to step back into the real world.

"So." Harrod looked at his brother. "All that rushing around trying to save you, and you were off having fun? That surprises me less than it should."

"Don't be such a wet fish. They were..." he sighed. "They were incredible. So beautiful and Gods, what they could do with their hands..."

Harrod choked on the last of his tea.

"Get your mind out of the gutter Harrod. They were just..." Martin sighed again. "I don't even know what they were doing, but they took good care of me."

"Apparently so," I said, trying to keep my face straight. "I'm glad to see you made it out in one piece at any rate. You didn't happen to eat or drink anything while you were there, did you?"

"No." Martin actually looked disappointed. "They didn't even offer."

That was unusual. The Fae had clearly enjoyed his company, though it was rare for a Fae to turn down any human. Normally, they would have plied any of their visitors with food and drink. One bite would give them the right to ownership, according to the law of the Otherworld.

Once it looked like Martin was more or less back in this world, I asked Harrod if he knew how much time we'd missed. He went to the kitchen and a brownie gave him the morning's paper. Five days had passed. Melanie would be starting to worry by now, though she knew where we had gone.

That was always a risk in crossing over; there was no way of knowing how time was passing in the mortal world. Sometimes you could visit the Otherworld, stay a year and return, only to find out it had been only mere minutes since you left. Of course, there were also many tales of the reverse—visitors who had made the trip and immediately returned into a world that was days, months, even years older.

All in all, five days wasn't a huge loss, but it did mean we'd have to hustle to get ready for the Gala. It was the following Friday—I needed a dress and all the fluff that goes with a formal outfit, and we had to make sure we were magically prepared too. I would have a lot of work to catch up on, and I needed to find out what happened to Gibble.

The way he looked when he'd left us weighed on me. In all the years we had been together, he'd never been anything but friendly. Grouchy sometimes, though that was often an act, but he had never frightened me. Though I often thought of him as my protector and my helper, truth was, he was family.

"Are you sure Opius will be there?" I asked Harrod. Jacoby's faced flashed into my mind, but I forced it away.

"Reasonably. There will be some kind of announcement, something to do with the treaty talks between the Talents and the humans. I don't know what his stance is regarding the matter but it's important enough that it should draw him out for the night." Harrod flipped through the pages of the newspaper as he spoke.

"Then what's the plan? If the invitation covers a partner I can go with you, can't I? I know I was usually able to get into events with my father without raising too many eyebrows."

"I think I can manage that." He didn't look at me, but smiled into his newspaper.

"Great." I sat for a moment, reality sinking in. "No, not great. Oh wow, out to catch a killer and I have nothing to wear."

Harrod laughed at that.

"Harrod, I'm serious! I don't even own a cocktail dress let alone something suitable for a Talented gala. Have the fashions changed much in the last fifteen years?"

"They're Talented, nothing ever changes for them. Don't worry. Today we rest, tomorrow we shop." Harrod grinned. "I know somewhere you can find the perfect attire."

I smiled thanks at him, Martin watching the exchange closely. Then, Harrod stretched and suggested we eat. Too tired to do much more, we sat and ate the sandwiches Martin had packed. It was a picnic lunch in an antique banquet hall. Ridiculous really.

Harrod offered me a room to sleep in and I gratefully accepted. I was exhausted and didn't relish the walk home. Martin found a spot for me and once we were alone, he gave me a smile.

"So, you've forgiven Harrod?"

"Yeah. We're all good." I returned a tired smile.

"I'm glad. He's a good man. A good friend."

"Yeah. He is."

With that, I crawled into a very plush four poster bed and went straight to sleep.

I woke in the wee hours of the morning, still weary but restless. A soft glow under the door told me someone was likely awake, so I padded out into the hallway. I found my way to a sitting room, where Martin sat alone. He looked up as I entered, looking far better than I felt.

"The sleeping princess awakes," he said, checking his watch. "You've had... sixteen hours. Feeling a bit better?"

I grunted at him and flopped into a chair. My head was pounding. He rang a tiny bell and asked the brownie that appeared to procure some coffee.

"Bring my potion box, too," he added.

I raised my eyebrows at him but had to laugh when the brownie returned with the coffee and a box of aspirin. "You read my mind," I said.

"No, I read your face. I'd heard the expression 'bear with a sore head' but I'd never realised how literal it was."

I considered throwing the box at his head but decided I needed it too much. I gulped down two tablets, *then* threw it.

Martin caught it with one hand and I wrinkled my nose at him irritably. He laughed back at me, then sobered.

"I didn't get a chance to thank you last night." His eyes dropped to the aspirin box as he turned it end over end, fiddling restlessly. "You saved my life, didn't you? They treated me well enough before you got there but if you hadn't managed to pass that test... I get the feeling bad things would have happened to me."

"Harrod tried, Martin. He tried so hard but—"

"Oh, I know. I saw it. His arm... Gods. I could see what was happening to me, I could feel it, but you did something. It was as though the pain—the fire, or the twisting—it would hurt so much, it was breaking my bones or cooking me from inside. Then you would... stop it." He sat back and shrugged. "I don't even know if it makes sense. I wasn't sure if Harrod's arm would get better, but it did. *You* did that, didn't you?"

"I don't know," I said softly. "I didn't know what I was doing. I just tried to block out the curse, refuse to believe it. It was just a mind trick, something to help me bear the pain. I didn't think it would actually do anything."

"They know." Martin looked at the floor.

"Know what?"

"That you're special. I could feel it when I was with them. They were really interested in you. When they were... ahem... while I was waiting for you to get there, they kept asking me questions. Questions that didn't make any sense." He'd flushed a deep shade of red when he'd mentioned his time with them. I tried not to wonder how they had passed the time.

"What did they ask?" Dread and confusion warred, but curiosity came out of top. "There's really nothing that interesting about me. Fae don't hate the half-bloods but they're not exactly overwhelmed by us either. They were probably trying to find out about the grail, or about Harrod. He's incredibly strong, even for a full blood Talent. They probably want him for something, it's how they work—they wouldn't bother with someone like me when Harrod's in the room."

"Harrod didn't hold on." His eyes met mine, full of gratitude.

"I told you, that wasn't his fault!"

"Yes I know. I don't blame him for it at all, but they *knew*, Emma, they knew *you'd* be able to do it. It's important. Do you remember what they said? 'You have two things you need'. Harrod was one of them. You and him. I don't know what happened, just that they wouldn't let you in until... I don't know, you'd kissed and made up or something. Before that, they were arguing. One asked what would happen if their little delay didn't work. The woman, the one who let us go? Said it didn't matter, that you're the key so that meant it would work out. A lot of it was fuzzy, like I'd been drinking, but I remember parts." He looked at me, struck by a thought. "Come to think of it, exactly how close *did* you two get on your way to rescue me?"

I snorted. "Pretty close to killing each other. We argued; damn near tore each other apart. Let off some steam, apologised, then forgave each other. That's it."

For some reason he didn't look convinced, but he didn't bring it up again. One of the brownies tapped on the door and entered. "Master Harrod is awake, sir. Will the lady be staying for breakfast?"

"Sure, Cym. Make it a decent spread, will you? We're starving."

"Yessir." The brownie bowed and scuttled off.

"The two of you have a house full of Otherworld servants but you fall over at one little boggart?"

"Boggarts aren't little, nor do they serve."

"Mine does. How'd Harrod end up with brownies anyway? I wouldn't pick him as the sort to have bought them." I assumed Harrod had brought them with him when he left the City. Brownies didn't have a familial bond like boggarts do, so he hadn't simply inherited them.

"They all owe him in one way or another." Martin waved away my look of horror. "Not like that, he's not making them work off debts or anything. He's helped them, freed a couple of them from mistreatment, that sort of thing. Harrod was one of the major campaigners against the ownership of Otherworld beings. This lot are all here out of pure loyalty."

"Wow." Ok, now I *really* felt like an ass for the assumptions I'd made about Harrod when we first met. I was saved from having to say anything else by the arrival of the man himself.

"Morning," he mumbled. He looked like he could use a few aspirin himself.

"Harrod... you look like hell." Martin said what I was too polite to say aloud.

"I feel it too," he said. "Didn't sleep. Bad dreams. There was a really angry dragon trying to bite my arm off..."

What we had been through the day before was enough to give anyone nightmares. Added to that, the Fae realms could get into your head in weird ways. I was more surprised that Martin and I had actually slept.

Cym returned a moment later to announce breakfast. We headed into the dining room to find a lavish spread, consisting of bacon, eggs, mushrooms and fat chunks of toasted bread. We fell to eating, hungry enough that conversation stopped for a while. Once I'd had my fill and topped it off with hot tea, I stood to go.

"I'd better get back; I need to check on Lenny. Hell, my shop's been closed for a week now. I've probably lost half my client base."

"I'm sure they won't mind," Harrod said.

"The shop is my livelihood, Harrod. If I don't sell, I don't eat. I don't even know if I've got anything TO sell, I've been so busy with all this..." It might not be on the level of serial killers and Otherworld adventures, but this could end up being a very real problem for me.

"No need to worry," Martin said. "Harrod's swimming in it. He'll cover your out of pockets."

I raised an eyebrow at him. "Kind of you to offer up someone else's money."

"No, really," Harrod said. "He's right and— "

He actually seemed eager but I put my foot down. "It's fine. Really. A couple of days won't bankrupt me, but I really do have to go." I drank the last of the tea—it was *really* good—and stood to leave. I looked around for my things but all I'd brought with me... was Gibble. *Right.* I took a steadying breath, then allowed Harrod to show me to the front door.

"I think I know someone who can help out with a gown,"

Harrod said. "For the Gala. If not, there are places we can try. I'll let you know later today?"

"Sure, thanks. I mean, I can buy a dress, I just don't know what I'm looking for. I haven't been to something like that since I was a child."

"Of course, it's really not a problem." Harrod stopped at the door. "Are you and I... we're good?"

"Yeah." My irritation vanished at his hesitant words. I smiled at him, then pulled him into a hug. "We're good."

∾

I reached the door to my empty tea shop. There was a sign on the door: 'Out Being Business-ing. Back Soon. Or Maybe Not.' *What on Earth?*

It only took a moment to check the wards. Before disabling them, I called out. "Barg? You there?" I felt silly calling for someone who probably wasn't there but a second later a small hobgoblin popped up out of nowhere.

Hobgoblins were larger than their demigoblin kin and smaller than traditional goblins. They were the most... unique, though. Raised in large clans with strong bonds to family but often obsessed with the human world, they straddled the bridge between the Other and this world like no other.

Bard saluted. "Yes, Lady! Barg is here, at your service!"

"Um, thanks." I glanced around but the street was otherwise empty. "You've been here the whole time?"

"Yes, Lady!" He snapped another salute. "House is safe! Lenny-Dog is well! You will tell Gibble I have paid my debt!"

"Uh... I'll tell Gibble you watched my house and fed my dog." He looked crestfallen. "I'll tell him you did a really good job, though?"

"Thank you, Lady!" Another salute.

I hid my smile. "You don't need to salute me. Especially not every time you speak."

"Yes, Lady!" He saluted again.

I shook my head and pulled my keys out. "How'd you get into... oh, right. Hobgoblin. Picked the lock?"

"Yes, Lady!" Salute. "You have very good locks!"

"Thanks. Oh, before I left I asked a friend to come over. You didn't run into her, did you?"

"Yes, Lady! Mellie-nanny did come to offer nourishing tributes to the Lenny-Dog. I did reassure her that Lenny-Dig did not require tributes, Lady! However, Mellie-nanny did wish to continue to personally placate the Lenny-Dog." He scratched his bristly chin. "After the first time we met, she did not scream very much."

"Ah. Well, thanks again. You can go now. Farewell." He stood there and blinked at me. I sighed. "Ok, you can come in and have something to eat, if I can find something. Only if you stop saluting, though. It's getting weird."

"Yes, Lady!" The hand jerked but stopped mid-way. Barg smiled sheepishly, jammed the offending hand in a pocket, then darted inside.

Lenny bounded towards me and I leaned down to throw my arms around him. He looked wonderful, even smelled good. "Hey, did you wash my dog?"

"Well... yes, Lady. You see, I got caught in rain shower. I was very cold. I thought, Barg, you need to warm up or you will freeze! So, I put the water in the big white inside-pond and I used the flower juices to make it smell nice. Lenny-Dog, he did not smell nice, so I made him swim in the inside-pond too." He looked bashful for a moment. "Lady," he whispered, "There is something wrong with the flower juices. It smelled very nice, but it made the water.... *fluffy*."

Trying not to laugh, I thanked him for his efforts. I dreaded to see the mess he'd left in my bathroom but it seemed he'd taken good care of Lenny at least. After a moment hunting through the kitchen,

I found some honey, crackers and a couple of apples that were about to turn. Barg jumped on them and they were gone in a blink.

"I will return to my duty now, Lady. Thank you for the fine refreshments."

"You can go, really. I'm home now and I won't be leaving again."

"I must wait for Gibble. I am not to leave until he returns!"

"Oh. Barg, something happened in the Otherworld. Gibble... changed. He got big and angry and... I'm not sure when he's coming back."

"Oh, Gibble went Wild? Yes, that is a boggart thing. He will return Lady! Do not fret! Gibble will unWild in the in-between and he will return to relieve Barg of duty!"

"Thank the Gods." I sagged with relief. "I didn't know what was happening, or if he's safe. It's normal then?"

"Yes, Lady. After many years bonded to a family, some boggarts will turn into mellow buttery-cakes. They must return to Wild-form to do some things—to use Wildmagic, or to take oaths, or to... Oh. Oh. Did Gibble find a *mate*?! Oh dear, oh dear, oh dear, that will take a *long* time. Barg must go, have things to do!" The hobgoblin hopped from one foot to the other in worry.

"No Barg, he didn't find a mate. I think he took an oath. He said we belonged to him. Three times. That was an oath?"

"Ah, yes Lady." He heaved a deep sigh of relief, hands dramatically to his chest. "Thrice said and will be done. He is bonded to you now, again. He must forevermore act as protector to all those he has claimed. It is a great honour, to be claimed twice by a boggart," He noticed my confusion and added, "Once to your family many lives ago, and now once to you. I do not think that happens often."

"Thank you, Barg. You may leave if you want. I will tell Gibble you've done a marvellous job." Crossing to the door I opened it expectantly.

The tiny creature bowed deeply, stepped through the door, waved, then popped out of existence. I closed the door, then jumped when he popped back a moment later, inside the shop.

"Ah, Lady... Barg almost forgot!"

He handed me a card, then disappeared again. I had no doubt he'd be around somewhere. Otherworldlings take debts *very* seriously. Doors, however, were more of an optional thing.

Absently taking my wand out I traced the lock shut again as I read the card. It was Greyson, asking if I could contact him. I winced.

It wasn't that I didn't want to talk to him, really. It would just be easier to explain the last few days after I had time to regroup. I picked up my phone to call him and breathed a sigh of relief when the call went to his message service.

"It's Emma, I just got your message. I've been... away. I need to get some sleep but I'll be in the shop tomorrow if you still need to talk."

I ended the call and looked around. I didn't have the energy to open the shop and besides, the day was half over. I went upstairs to inspect the damage. Not too bad. The bathroom smelled of cheap body wash and what looked like every towel I owned was piled in a corner covered in dog hair. The floor was still wet, too.

Well, no rest for the wicked. I put the towels in the wash, mopped the floor and cleaned the mirror, which had comical pixie faces drawn on it in brown eyeliner. I checked the drawers—messier than normal but otherwise ok—threw my toothbrush in the bin (Gods knew where it had been over the last few days) and did the same to the razor when I realised it was out of place. Yech.

I was tired down to my bones by the time I'd finished. That was an after-effect of our journey and I knew it would hang around for a few days, like bad jetlag. I checked the wards that now permanently adorned my bedroom, then crawled into bed. Lenny joined me, snuggling up and licking my face. I was asleep in minutes.

CHAPTER NINETEEN

Greyson was waiting when I opened the shop the next day. I let him in, leaving him to entertain himself while I served the influx of customers. It was some time before I had the chance to talk to him.

After closing for a week, my regular customers were eagerly waiting both for their teas, and to find out where I'd been. I tried to keep the details sparse, but rumours had already spread about my trip to the Otherworld and Gibble 'going Wild' and the oath he had made. Eventually, I had to ask them to stop talking about it.

Eventually, the stream of sales slowed to a trickle and I managed to break away to speak with Greyson, who had stayed patiently to one side until I was free.

"Emma." He thrust out a hand to accompany his greeting and I shook it wearily. "I just wanted to check in on you, I saw the shop was closed and I was worried. The goblin said he'd take a message but that was two days ago."

"He's a hobgoblin," I explained. "Goblins are bigger and more likely to eat you." That wasn't technically true, but I was sick of mortals not bothering to learn the names of the creatures that spent so much time in our world.

"Hobgoblin. Right, sorry. Anyway, I thought I'd update you on our progress. We've had more than one source confirm the perpetrator is a Talent."

Bloody genius, this one. I shut down the uncharitable line of thought quickly – Greyson was only doing his best with what he had. "So you think we're on the right track?" I broke away from our conversation to see to a customer. "Sorry, Joseph, I'm out of Mindsharp. I have Awaken or Remembrance if either of those will do?"

"It's hard to pin down fact from rumour but it stacks up so far." Greyson continued on as I wrapped a box and handed it over to Joseph, one of my few mortal customers.

"Anything more on Opius?" I asked.

"Yeah, we've heard his name mentioned." Greyson scribbled down a note. "If it's him, we've no chance of getting to him, even for questioning. Seems he's right up there in rank."

"I'm going to try and get a look at him soon. Yes, I've got three boxes. No, that's it, I'm afraid." The door swung open again and I sighed. The stream of customers was never-ending today. "There's a gala coming up and Harrod said he can get me in."

"You mentioned him before. That's Harrod... Umbers, right? He's that Talent living this side of the Wall?"

"That's him."

"Ah. The two of you are...?" He left the question hanging.

"That's four chips Nuft. Thanks." I turned back to Greyson. "Not a chance, I just met him. He came to me looking for information, why?"

Greyson coughed, looked away, and blushed. "Just curious. Tell me about this gala."

"There's an announcement coming, I'm not sure what it is. You know there's been a change in government?" I wiped the counter as Greyson nodded. "Right, so we're going to attend the gala, get a look at the guys face, see who he's aligning himself with, and leave."

"You'll be safe there?" Greyson asked the question with unexpected urgency. "A lot of powerful people go to those things, and most of them are pillocks. I don't want you at risk, you hear?"

His concern was equal parts sweet, and annoying. "It'll be fine. Harrod will be there, and we'll be in public the whole time. No one would dare make a fuss at a gala event."

Four more customers walked in and then another two. Greyson waved a farewell at me, not wanting to interrupt as he made his departure.

The following days passed quickly. I worked my fingers to the bones boxing up teas, tracing spells on my special brews late into the night and early in the mornings. Days were filled with customer sales. I had been missed, apparently. Word had spread on the Otherworld grapevine that I had returned, and even some of my less-frequent clientele seemed to be stocking up lest I disappear into the Other again. My supplies were barely keeping up with the demand. It was all the harder for not having Gibble. Normally, he would help with the boxing, tidy up and keep things in order. He'd sell when I needed him to and even his mere presence would stop squabbles from breaking out, which was wont to happen when the exact wrong combination of Otherworld denizens were in the shop at the same time.

Strangely, despite the busy atmosphere and more creatures packing the shop than normal, the peace wasn't broken. I found out why when I saw Tilke, a kobold with a deep hatred for gnomes on his way in, right when three gnomish customers were making their purchases.

"Uh, guys? You'd better scram. There's a kobold coming down the street."

The gnomes looked up in fright and proceeded to stuff their purchases into a sack. They weren't fast enough. Tilke opened the door just as they reached it and I braced for a tussle. It would never get too violent but a creature of that size in a tiny shop like mine could wreak havoc just by sneezing. To my surprise, Tilke stepped back to let them pass, though he growled and snapped at their backs as they left.

"Thank you," I said to him.

"What, for not squashing tiny thieves in your shop?"

"Yes. That." I'd never had a theft (that I knew of) but knew the little creatures had a reputation for light-fingeredness.

"Ah. You are safe from the petty squabbles of our kind now, if not from thieving hands. The boggart has claimed you—only the foolish would brave the wrath he would bring down if they were seen to be disturbing your peace."

"You heard about that too, huh?"

Tilke nodded slowly. "Such a claim is no small thing, and word travels fast in the Other."

I sold him the teas he requested—two boxes for light mental enhancement (kobolds are quite a scholarly race) and one for language translation, one of my rarer blends. He paid his chips and left me to my busy shop.

On Friday afternoon, just a week before the Talent Gala, I was due back at Harrod's to meet a seamstress. We were cutting it a bit fine but he assured me she could have it ready on time. He'd made the reservation late enough that I wouldn't have to close the shop early. After shooing off the last dawdling shoppers, I locked the front door and raced upstairs to shower and change. I hoped the fitting wouldn't take long—I still had to box up more stock after I got back to account for the extra sales I'd been making.

I got to Harrod's by mid-afternoon. When I arrived, he shepherded me straight out the door. We took the Bentley, this time driven by a short, furred creature. I had no idea what it was... or how it saw over the steering wheel to drive the monstrosity of a car.

We reached the Wall in a few short minutes. *Of course*, I thought. This was a gala—Even London's High Street fell a bit short of the dress requirements. Harrod wound a window down and nodded at two guards standing duty. They waved him through instantly. Clearly, they recognised him.

Normally, papers would be presented and for low-born Talents or half-bloods like myself, details recorded. I was reminded yet again of the rank Harrod held inside the City, though it was becoming less intimidating over time.

The car slipped through the cobbled streets. I had been inside the City before, but not for a long time. Buildings crowded together—there had been little room for expansion of the Inner City once the mortals started building outside. Thanks to the use of magic, the Inner City was able to grow by twisting streets into themselves and creating space in a way that would make a mortal physicist question everything he knew. Over time, Talent architects cobbled together old existing buildings with... well, more of the same.

Talents in the Inner City had been here for generations. They eschewed modern technology and aesthetics, so the entire City was still comprised of materials that resembled something from the Middle Ages brought back to life. The result was something that, when compared with orderly Outer-London terraces and streets, looked somewhat like a dogs' breakfast. Not that I'd say that out loud to a Talent of course.

The scenery changed as we entered what looked to be a commercial district. Small signs flapped in the breeze in a way that was just enough to grab the attention. Talented folk were old-fashioned in many ways, but in others—such as the art of marketing to a limited, saturated market—they had had to embrace more modern techniques.

Glass windows with trade goods—herbs, wands, books, food and clothing all were displayed amongst strategically placed glow lights, dancing figures, miniature fireworks and more. It was stunning. The scent of fresh baked bread and roasted meat permeated the car long before we reached a building marked as The Lords Inn. As we passed it, my stomach cramped in hunger and I ached for a plate of food with a cold beer to wash it down. After we passed, the feeling dissipated, around the same time that I remembered I had already eaten and that I hate the taste of beer. Perhaps the high and mighty Talented aren't above cheap tricks to make a sale.

The car pulled up next to a side street and Harrod motioned me out. I stepped out, feeling self-conscious in my jeans and blouse. I expected the women within the City to cleave to the old fashion styles, but on looking around, I saw a few my own age dressed in casual street clothes. That would have been unheard of fifteen years ago when I was last here.

We stepped through a doorway underneath a small sign that simply said 'Bee's'. Inside, full sized models of humans, Fae, and other more civilised creatures spun in a dance, circling the room. The bodies were transparent, with vague features, allowing full attention to be given to the ball gowns they wore. Blues, purples, and pinks seemed to be the current fashion, with the occasional daisy-yellow making an appearance. As the figures spun, the dresses changed. Most were lavish, dripping in expensive stones and crafted with magical thread that rippled, glowed or sparkled. There were a few dresses of a simpler nature, but they were no less beautiful. These relied on the drape of fabric and perfect cut to show their craftsman-ship. One look at these and I knew I was not only right out of my comfort zone, but my price range as well.

I cleared my throat and spoke to Harrod in a low voice. "Harrod, you know I'm not... I can't afford anything from here."

"Hush," he said. "I told you—this one is on me. I need you there with me, and you need to be able to blend in with the other guests. This is a necessary expense and one I'm well prepared to cover."

"You realise it's not just the dress, right? I'll need shoes and hosiery and um, jewellery." I wasn't about to give him the chance to offer to pay for a new set of underclothes—which, looking at plunging backs and open sides, I'd need.

"I may be a man but I'm not completely clueless about ladies' fashions. Bee provides everything, the shoes, the hair accessories, even...." He coughed and blushed. Dammit, he was buying my underwear.

Ok then. I let the small feeling of anticipation fill me. I'd never, *never* owned a dress like one of these. Even in my childhood, attending court with my father was usually a sombre affair. My garb had been restricted to that suitable for a child and while pretty, didn't compare to these wonders. Despite my dislike for Talent Lords in general, I couldn't deny their flair for the beautiful.

A woman swept from a side room and I froze when I realised she was Fae. Her tall, lithe figure practically glowed with Otherworldliness and her delicately folded ears twitched when she saw me.

"Emmeline! Oh, my dear, I've been *so* hoping to see you. Are you here for a dress? Please say you'll be at the Gala!" A tinkling laugh erupted from her dew-drop mouth. She spun and put a hand on Harrod's arm.

He gave me a briefly confused glance, then smiled at the gorgeous Fae. "Yes, Bee. Emma needs something. I hope we haven't left it too close?"

"Harrod, you insult me!" She didn't sound insulted. In fact, she sounded like she wanted to lick him. I bristled a little at the way she hung off him, then berated myself for it.

Bee turned to me, one finger on her chin in a pose that was clearly meant to show her deep in seductive thought. Fae dripped sex appeal when they were happy and Bee was positively joyous. "I know exactly what you need. You don't find green objectionable? Of course you don't, it suits you perfectly. I'll bring it to you before the Gala. You'll need help getting ready of course, I doubt Harrod has the skill to get one such as yourself dressed for your debut in society."

"Debut?" Panic flared and I backed away. "Oh no, this is just—

Bee would have none of it. "My dear, you really don't know how much society pines for one like yourself. So fresh, so focused. I promise, you will become a fixture around here. Most will welcome it."

"I somehow doubt that..."

"Don't worry about the traditionalists. You will give them a run for their money, I'm sure. Now, run along and I'll see you in a couple of days."

"What about the dress? And..." I glanced over at Harrod, who was staring out a window, and lowered my voice. "How did you know my name?"

"Oh darling, you've been away far too long. I am Fae! The dress will be just perfect, I assure you."

She ushered us out of the shop. Apparently, her skill extended to the ability to create a perfect fit without taking a single measurement. Of course it did. She was Fae.

The night of the Gala, I arrived at Harrod's early. I was hoping to get there early enough to settle my nerves with a cup of tea before Bee was due, but when Harrod showed me through to the sitting room, she was already there.

"Oh, Bee. I'm not late, am I?"

"No dear, I wanted to come by early to meet Harrod's little brother. I've heard he's quite delicious."

I coughed to cover my discomfort over her particular phrasing. "Probably not the word I'd use. Where is he?"

"Definitely not the word I'd use." Harrod seemed unsure what to think of Bee's interest in Martin. "He's out, I'm not sure where. He said he had an errand and was supposed to be back before you both arrived."

As he spoke, there was a clatter at the front door. A moment later, Martin strode in carrying flowers. He stopped when he saw us, then backpedalled, motioning with his head for Harrod to join him. Bee raised a delicate eyebrow at me and I shrugged. After a few moments' wait, the two men came back into the room, each carrying a bunch of flowers. Harrod handed one to me and I looked at it quizzically.

"It's for tonight. Because you're my date. Apparently—" he shot a glower in his brother's direction, "it's a long-standing tradition, though I suppose it could have been planned a little better."

I took the flowers, blushing. I held them awkwardly, unsure what to do with them as Martin approached Bee. He stared at her like a deer caught in the headlights.

"Well, well, who is this? Harrod, why didn't you tell me how adorable he is?"

Harrod coughed. "Bee, he's not up for..."

"Oh, he *is*. He's played with our kind before, hasn't he? And what is your name, precious?"

"Martin," he said in a hoarse whisper.

"Martin, you and I shall be getting to know each other quite well, I think."

"Bee..." Harrod's voice had a hard edge to it now.

"Yes, Yes, I think I'd like that." Martin seemed to have gotten over his momentary stupor. Bee reached a hand out and touched his cheek. His mouth parted, and he leaned towards her. Harrod cleared his throat and she pulled away with a laugh. Martin stood for another moment, then found a seat, not taking his eyes off the stunningly beautiful Fae.

I cleared my throat. "Martin, I spoke to Melanie earlier. She said something about a date to the theatre?"

"Hmm? Oh. Not with me. She let me down very gently, but I do believe I was dumped. Positively heartbroken I am. I think I need cheering up. A chap can't just go around with a broken heart, you know." He gave Bee a sly smile. The flirting was a bit much, but at least he seemed in control of himself now. His initial reaction to Bee had worried me—I wasn't sure if his treatment in the Otherworld would have a lasting effect.

"I don't think that's a good idea. Not with this one." Harrod didn't pay any attention to the pouty look Bee threw him.

Pulling me up from her seat she said, "Off we go, my dear. These boys don't need to be around for this. In fact, I believe you mortals like to be mostly alone when undressing, am I right?"

"Yes!" I replied emphatically, face burning at the thought of stripping down in front of anyone. A brownie—I think it was Cym—appeared to take the flowers we both still held and showed us to a room.

There was a large trunk placed on the bed. She cracked it open and pulled something out, without letting me see inside. Passing me a small parcel, she gestured for me open it. Underwear. Sheer, skimpy underwear. Clearly she didn't want her handy work undone by any peeking straps or panty lines.

"Put these on, then we can get to work." It wasn't a request, so I swallowed hard and nodded.

She turned away just long enough for me to change into the light underwear. Despite its fragile appearance, it fit well and held me in where it needed to. And it wasn't see-through, thank goodness. That didn't lessen the amount of blood rushing to my cheeks while I stood in front of a stranger, feeling even more naked that I actually was. Without letting me dress further, Bee sat me at the antique dresser in the room and started on my hair. I hadn't expected that—I'd been going to pull it into a simple up-do. Bee had other plans, extravagant ones.

Rather than use a comb or a hairbrush, she ran her fingers through my hair. As she pulled, my hair straightened out, all the usual kinks and curls falling out into smooth tresses. She twisted it up, leaving the front portion free, then set to work. She pulled out a section of hair as thick as my finger. She ran her fingers along it and I felt a light tugging on my scalp. When she reached the end a bare moment later, it was intricately braided with a tendril of fine flowers running through it. She repeated this several times across the front of my hair. Then, she moved to the back, pulling it straight and then springing it up into perfectly formed, loose curls.

Once she was done she wove the braids through to the back, so they held my hair off my neck but still let the bulk of my curls swing down past my shoulders. She fussed at it for some time, redoing sections that didn't meet with her approval. Finally, she gave a smile of satisfaction. She placed her hands over my head and muttered a spell of holding to set it all in place.

She turned me around, then started on my face. She worked with brushes and powders and flowers and tiny sparkling things. I held my eyes closed as she worked, to save losing one of them. Her hands glided over my face with soft fingers and a sweet smelling cream. She pressed tiny button-like items onto my face, mumbling a word with each one to hold it in place.

As she worked, I tried not to squirm. I hadn't realised the degree of effort she'd intended on going to. Either she just loved to play dress up, or this gala was a really serious event.

When Martin had first described the invitation, he'd made it seem like one of the typical displays of wealth and power that occurred on an almost weekly basis within the Inner City. Now, however, I was getting nervous. With the announcement regarding Talented relations with the outside world Harrod had mentioned, combined with Bee's extraordinary attention, it seemed likely we were headed to a Grand Gala, an event at which all the Talent Lords and Ladies would be present.

I was sure I wouldn't be recognised. Ok, I desperately hoped I wouldn't. I was sure to run into at least one Talent Lord who had associated with my father – or who hated him. Though I didn't really know what his standing was, I knew he had at least a few enemies. No blood feuds or anything that would flow down onto his descendants I was sure, but it could become awkward. The only thing that stopped me from refusing to go was knowing my sisters were unlikely to attend—they rarely came to the City, instead preferring the warmer climate and relaxed society of America.

Then, as if my nerves weren't shattered enough, I remembered the dancing...

At a regular event there were few demands, and the evening had a casual feel. At a Grand Gala, security was tight, and it was expected that everyone would participate in the planned itinerary, including the dancing. I was passable, but only just, and the thought of trying to waltz around with several powerful eyes on me made my stomach writhe with anxiety.

After what seemed an eternity, Bee finished painting my face. I opened my eyes, but before I had a chance to inspect her work, she pulled me over to the bed. Bee opened the trunk again and pulled out a pale, shimmering dress of green and ivory.

"Now dear, stand like this. Just move your arm a little... yes, perfect. Now hold still."

She waved, and the dress floated into the air. It slithered around my body, fitting perfectly and securing itself at the back. It was, in a word, stunning. The dress was translucent white, with tiny tendrils of green running through it. The delicacy of the design made portions of the dress throw hues of forest green. It was adorned with tiny white butterflies, trailing down from one shoulder and across the bodice. As I moved, their wings opened and closed, making the dress appear to ripple in a breeze. I turned to the mirror. My face was done in natural tones, but if I tilted my face a certain way, a light sparkle touched my skin. Rather than paint me with bright, striking colours Bee had opted for a subtle look. A nymph-like trail of flowers started on my cheekbone and ran around my eye and up past my temple. I turned my head and caught a glimpse of tiny, fluttering wings amongst my tresses.

I spun, trying to see every angle in the tiny mirror. The girl in the mirror was beautiful, so light and poised. All my previous anxiety was gone... I realised with a start I'd been enchanted. Not just stunning, the gown had been woven with a spell that would grant me the grace I'd require to not only survive the evening but do justice to my partner, a high-ranking Talent Lord.

Behind me, Bee was positively glowing with pride at her handiwork. She led the way downstairs.

I glided down behind her, filled with confidence. Bee met me at the bottom, placed a hand on my arm and together, we stepped up to the entrance to the sitting room. The two men looked up.

"You're... You look... I mean, your dress..." Harrod swallowed. "It's very nice."

"Very nice? Nice? Are you completely blind? She looks incredible! Gods Harrod, *nice* is not what you call a woman when she comes into a room looking like that." Martin looked at me in awe. He clearly hadn't expected such a striking change. Colour rose in my cheeks, unable to be suppressed by the enchantment soothing my nerves.

"May I present... The Lady Emmeline Myrwenna Ysolde Beaumarchais."

I froze, the words like a knife plunged into my chest and twisted. All traces of the enchantment vanished.

Harrod looked up in shock. I stood, trembling and white, all my previous poise and grace gone. Bee laughed like a child who has played a prank on a sibling at the expression on Harrod's face. Then, she looked back and saw me.

Everything was still.

My head spun and I realised I'd stopped breathing. Forcing myself to gasp some air in, I carefully made my way over to a seat. Bee rushed to my side, clasping my arm. "You didn't tell them?" she murmured.

"I don't go by that name anymore. I'd appreciate if you don't use it again please." My voice was hoarse, betraying emotion I'd rather keep well hidden.

"Emma?" Harrod's voice was unsure.

"We need to go," I said. "The last thing I need is to draw attention by being late."

"Emma, why didn't you say something?" Harrod took a step toward me but I turned my head away.

"Please, not now."

He paused. "Later, then. I'll go and call for the car."

After he left, Bee looked at me with serious eyes. "You can't hide it. They'll all find out eventually."

Eyes burning with unshed tears, I turned away. I strode out of the room and waited for Harrod by the front door. He came to stand next to me after a moment and before long, the Bentley was purring on the sidewalk. He helped me inside, my arms full of dress so that I wouldn't sully it on the ground. I turned my head as we took off, looking out the window and away from his eyes.

"Emma, I'm sorry. I had no idea. I wouldn't have made you come tonight if I'd known who you are."

"Why does that make a difference to you?" I asked, my voice hard with unshed tears.

"Everyone there would know your father's name. You might be faced with questions, I don't want to put you through that after... well, you know."

"You mean they'll want to know how he died and why I didn't. If I knew the man who killed him, or why he did it. Yes, I bloody well know what I'm up for, Harrod. It doesn't matter, though. If Bee hadn't told you no one would have any idea who I am. It's old news, people won't remember if they're not reminded of it."

"Em..." Harrod blew out a slow breath. "*Everybody* knew Lucius. It's his work that got us where we are tonight, the fight that he started changed the entire community, forever."

I frowned. "What fight? My father was a businessman."

I looked over at Harrod. He was looking at me with concern and wonder. "Emma, your father was one of the key leaders in opening the doors of our world to others. The Fae, the mortals... He's the reason Abnett got elected, it all started with him. If not for Lucius, we wouldn't be nearly as close as we are."

I was cold inside. "I can't deal with this now. I can't."

"Emma, you're about to walk into a room full of people, very powerful people." Harrod tugged at my arm, forcing me to face him. "Some of them thought your father was a god, most just thought he was a nuisance, but more than a few wanted him dead. If any of them were involved and thought you knew about it... Ah hell."

Harrod sat back in the seat and rubbed his face. He looked almost as worried as when Martin was taken. "I'm sorry Emma, I know this is the last thing you want to talk about but... They said you found him. If you know who—

"I didn't find him, Harrod." Pent up emotion overrode the need to keep my secrets safe, secrets I had held onto for far too long. "I was *there*. I was there the whole time. I watched them kill my father in front of me and there was nothing I could do to stop them."

"Oh, Emma. I'm so sorry. Gods, you were what, eleven?" He stopped and I knew the question he was too afraid to ask. It was one I'd asked myself a million times.

"You want to know how I survived, don't you?"

Harrod frowned, then nodded. Throat tight, I told him what I remembered. "We were in the dining hall, having dinner. Nothing seemed unusual, until Father stood, pulled his wand out then told me to run and hide. He must have been alerted by a ward, but... it was too late. A man came in and traced a spell. He was faster, I guess. Father fell to the floor, unconscious. The spell didn't affect me like it should have, I knew what it was supposed to do but it didn't work. I fell down anyway and peeked through my eyelashes while I pretended to be asleep. He killed my father while I watched. When he was done, he wiped his knife on the carpet next to me. I was so afraid, I thought I was going to vomit. He didn't even check to see if I was awake, he just left. I stayed like that, on the floor next to Father's body until Gibble came the next morning."

I could see Harrod's reflection in the window I stared out of. His eyes were on me, and his hand reached for mine. He dropped it back when I made a small movement away.

I didn't deserve his sympathy. Gibble was the only person who knew what I'd seen, the only one who knew my guilty secret. The few who knew I had been there assumed I had been unconscious. Gibble was the only one who knew I could have done something to help. I could have saved my father.

"Do you know who it was?" Harrod asked.

"No. I tried looking, a little, when I came back to London. There wasn't much to go on, though, and I had no contacts. Morwenna had already left the country. Aveline never liked me much and after Father died... she told me never to come back. I don't blame her, really." I shrugged, trying to believe I didn't really care what she thought even after all these years.

"You were a child, Emma. It wasn't your fault. If you had tried to stop him you'd have gotten yourself killed too. You couldn't have saved your father no matter how hard you tried." Harrod's voice was soft.

"Because I was a child, or a half-blood?" I snapped at him.

"Because he was a trained assassin." Harrod didn't seem offended at my words. "Emma, I didn't work with your father directly, but I know what he did. He rallied the Talented to stand up for the rights of Otherworld servants. He exposed the bribery and corruption behind the half-blood orphanage. They were working children as slaves, Emma, and your father put a stop to it. He went up against some of the most powerful men and women in the Inner City and he took them down. These people don't mess around and they don't do their own dirty work. You're lucky to be alive."

His words rocked me. Although I knew Father abhorred the elitist attitude of many of his peers, he'd never told me what his 'business' meetings were about. Looking back, I could see that it was unusual, even the way he'd taken and introduced me to so many people. He had always sent me away for the important discussions though and as a child, I hadn't known any better.

"There's something else." Harrod shifted uncomfortably as he spoke. "Aveline will be there tonight."

Shit. Even after this long, I doubted my own sister wouldn't recognise me.

"You can turn back." Harrod reached for my hand again and this time, I let him. "I can take you back to the house and I can go alone."

"No, I need to see this man." I didn't say that I needed to know he wasn't the man I thought he might be. "If he's been watching me, I might recognise him." I hoped I didn't – Jacoby wasn't someone I was particularly close to, but the thought that I had entertained such a monster in my shop filled me with horror.

Harrod sighed. "Well then. I don't think you'll be in any great danger tonight, even if you *are* recognised. It will be crowded, we may not even see Aveline if she's there. The proceedings will be watched closely and those currently in power are sympathisers, so if they realise who you are they'll be especially careful to keep an eye on you. We can sneak out early, just as soon as we catch a glimpse of Opius." He hesitated. "You don't think he's targeting you because of your father, do you?"

"No." I hoped not anyway. "The other victims didn't have any ties to my family, or to the movement. They were just... people. I think he came across me by accident, or the same way he found them. I'm not special Harrod, I'm not connected to my family anymore and I'm... there's no reason for anyone to hate me."

Harrod looked at me carefully. Finally, he nodded then looked away.

"Martin was right, by the way. You look incredible."

I blushed. "Thanks."

Chapter Twenty

We arrived at the venue, a lavish palace near the centre of the Inner City. Well-dressed brownies greeted us at the entrance, then passed us over to a faske to be admitted into the ball-room. We were led through a majestic doorway as our names were announced.

"Introducing Harrod Reginald Umbers, Third Lord of the Fifth Family, and his partner Emmeline Beaumarchais, Third Daughter of the Ninth Lord of the Twelfth Family."

"Well, there goes the hope no one will recognise you," Harrod muttered. "How the bloody hell did they find out?"

A collective gasp went through the room and nearby heads turned our way. Thankfully the announcement hadn't been loud—most of the room would have missed it, but I had no doubt that within minutes every person in the room would know I was here. We descended the stairs into the ballroom. My dress floated around me, catching the eye of more than one person. The ladies around me were dressed in extravagant fabrics, dripping with jewels. My dress stood out not only for its relative simplicity, but for its elegance and beauty. I not only reached the fashion standards of the Talented Gala, I exceeded them.

Harrod led me straight to the dance floor. No one here stood on the sidelines, it just wasn't done. I stepped carefully on feet that were just a little unsteady, nerves vying to take control. When the next song started, however, my anxiety melted away.

Harrod was a wonderful dancer. His technique was not only perfect, he had that special trick that allowed him to lead an inexperienced dancer such as myself. With his guidance and Bee's spell, my steps were smooth and followed his easily. I suspected he was holding back an impressive amount of skill, but he just smiled at me as we sailed across the floor. The dancing portion would last until after the highest of the nobility had entered and had danced several rounds themselves. We had little chance for conversation with others so for now, I could relax and enjoy the experience.

If anyone could create a spectacle, it was a bunch of rich nobles with nothing better to do than impress other rich nobles. The room we were in was adorned with intricate paintings from floor to ceiling, figures that moved and sailed with the dancers themselves. The images gliding across the walls and ceiling were not only human but Fae and Otherworld creatures alike. Only the powerful, beautiful breeds of course—no lesser being would grace these walls.

The paintings covered all walls but one, which was adorned by large windows and terraces leading out onto the gardens. As we swept past them, I saw glimpses of lights and tables outside. It seemed this was to be an outdoor affair then. Talent events had no need to worry about such trivial things as wet grass or impending rain. They had enough skill at their disposal—their own or hired specialists—to whisk all that away with the wave of a wand.

The dancing lasted for what seemed an eternity... yet, when the music stopped I wished it had lasted longer. I was caught in the magic of the night, with my beautiful dress, lavish surroundings and, if I was honest with myself, a rather handsome man with his arms wrapped around me. That last thought was a dangerous one, but it wasn't easily dismissed. We weren't here for fun, I had a job to do. So sue me if it was an enjoyable one.

After the musicians ceased playing there was a short period of respite. Harrod mingled as his station demanded, introducing me to each person he spoke to. I wondered if the order of entrance and the dancing had some ulterior purpose—those of the lowest rank had been dancing the longest. Those unlucky souls were breathing a little quickly and showed some fatigue and there was no place to sit and rest. I admired their stamina. I was grateful for our late entry—my feet were already beginning to ache, despite the perfectly fitted shoes Bee had provided.

As we spoke to one man whom Harrod had greeted warmly, I heard him ask in a low voice if Opius had attended. He was told yes, he had, but due to his advanced... condition, he had been exempt from the ballroom ceremonies. As the man walked off, a woman's voice from behind made my blood freeze.

"I see the rumours are true. You've found a little pet to further your cause, Umbers. Mind, she bites."

I couldn't talk past the lump in my throat. My chest constricted and I almost stumbled as Harrod turned to see who spoke. I didn't need to look. That voice had been burned into my memory since childhood.

"Aveline." Harrod nodded to her without turning around. He took my arm and steered me away, trying to shield me from her sight. It didn't work.

"I thought you'd have more class than that, my friend." Avelines biting, nasal voice hadn't changed since she was a young woman. "You've won your little battle for the seat, no need to use cheap tricks to further your cause."

"Tricks, Aveline?" Harrod spoke smoothly enough that you almost wouldn't notice the sharp edge to his words. "At least I didn't try to seduce half the lords in the City in an attempt to turn their vote."

"It's a pity the ballots were silent." Aveline clicked her tongue. "I would love to see the look on your face when you find out which of the Lords I own."

"Harrod my dear, so wonderful to see you. Emmeline, you look divine! Just stunning. Of course, no one would expect less for your formal debut, would they?" Speaking just as if she hadn't been responsible for my garb herself, Bee smoothly inserted herself in front of Aveline and clasped my arm. "Come, my love, people are just dying to speak with you."

She pulled me away and I let out a sigh of relief as I went to be introduced to her friends, leaving Harrod behind to deal with my sister. Bee announced me to a small gathering of Lords, Ladies and Fae, all of whom gushed over me like a long-lost friend. Though nothing of importance was spoken of, most of them made some small reference to my father—saying he was greatly missed or had been a real asset to the Talented community. Nothing was mentioned of my sisters.

Just as Harrod found me and was about to lead me away, the large glass doors leading outside all opened at once. The ballroom lights dimmed slightly, and those outside brightened to lead us out. We exited the room, with all the poise and decorum one would expect from a gaggle of nobility. Women whispered behind fans and men coughed, stating that surely so and so's ball had been quite comparable, if not quite so populated.

Harrod and I reached the threshold to the garden and a little piske popped up to lead us to our seat. The gardens were interspersed with large round tables, and paths strewn with white flowers between them. Despite the soft look of the grass, my feet were as steady as walking on concrete, suggesting there was more magic here than I could see.

We reached our table while it was still empty. The faske seated us, placing napkins in our laps and glasses on the table. It wasn't long before we were joined by two men, announced as Bartholomew and Stanley. Stanley did a double take upon seeing Harrod and broke into a wide smile.

"Harrod, you old miscreant! What brings you out of the slums?"

Harrod rose and clasped Stanley's arm. "Couldn't get a date? That's a first."

"Well... actually I've jumped ship, so to speak. I'm afraid it's somewhat serious."

Harrod snorted. "You've never held down a relationship for more than a week."

"Actually," Bartholomew interjected. "It's coming on a year now."

Harrod looked thrilled at this and hugged his friend. "Congratulations! A year? I'm sorry, I really have been out of touch, haven't I?"

"Yeah, you have." Stanley's voice had a serious edge but it was quickly dismissed. "This is Barty, anyway. Harrod here is my old partner in crime, from back..." He shot a glance at the others at the table. "Well, back in the day."

Bartholomew, or 'Barty' as he was clearly not happy to be called, looked at Harrod, then me, then back at Harrod, slyly cocking his eyebrow. The interchange was interrupted by the third couple, an elderly man and woman. Without waiting for an introduction, the three men at the table rose and bowed, Harrod gently nudging my arm. I followed suit with a hasty curtsy, hoping I didn't look the fool. Clearly these guests were important. The piske accompanying them spoke.

"Introducing the Illustrious Grand Master Dyson Undridge and his Lady, the Duchess Columbine Undridge."

Their names were familiar to me—Dyson and Columbine were a power couple in the City. They were involved in multiple dealings with those outside the Inner City, so I hoped this didn't make for an awkward dinner. I had assumed I wouldn't be expected to make small talk, but the Duchess turned to me as soon as she was seated.

"Emmeline how are you, my dear? It was quite the surprise to hear you introduced with Harrod this evening. Tell me, how are your sisters?"

I flailed for a brief moment, unsure what to say. Harrod rescued me.

"Duchess Columbine, this is Emma. She's my partner this evening. Emma, Collie and I have known each other for some time. I think you'll like her." I wasn't sure which of us that last bit was meant for.

I smiled politely. I didn't think Harrod knew the kind of people I liked—stuffy nobles whose first concern was family rank didn't rate that highly on my list.

A faske, flightless cousin to the piskes, came by with a tray of champagne flutes and wine glasses. He placed a drink in front of each person without asking preference, until he reached me. "What would my lady prefer?"

"The pink, please," I said in a small voice. The last time I'd attended a Talent social event, I hadn't been old enough to drink. There was no set age within the society like there was outside the Walls, but there was a general, if flexible consensus that twelve was the absolute minimum. Soon after Father died, I was torn from what little interaction I'd had with his people, so despite my upbringing, there were still large parts of Talented society I'd never been exposed to. I hoped the wine wasn't awful, or terribly intoxicating.

"Excellent choice," the Faske said, placing a glass in front of me. I gently moved it to one side. The drinks wouldn't be touched until the opening toast. Harrod was watching me, clearly evaluating my knowledge of the correct procedures. He smiled when he saw I was looking at him, then quickly squeezed my hand under the table.

Gods, this was nerve-wracking. If I slipped up, even something so small as to take a sip of my drink too early or address someone highly ranked the wrong way, it would reflect on him badly. I knew he still networked a lot with those inside the City and I didn't want to cause him any embarrassment.

A hush fell over the gardens, then a voice boomed forth.

"Ladies and Gentleman, Nobles and Talents. I present to you our great lord and keeper of the traditions, High Master Garedd Jameson Abnett."

There was a smattering of applause. I turned to the head table set up at the front of the garden, only a short distance from where we sat. Together with the other Gala guests I raised my glass in a toast to the new High Master, then took a careful sip of my wine. It tasted sweet but had a sharpness to it that tickled my nose. I'd tasted worse.

A bell rang out across the lawn, sounding over the chatter that now filled the evening air. Abnett waited a moment for the rustles of conversation died down, then began to speak. He spoke for a long time. A *really* long time.

He gave a short history of Talent, from the time the first people were blessed with power by the Fae, until the more recent agreements with the mortals outside the Inner City. With little inflection in his voice, he touched on 'a slight unrest' that changed the way the unTalented were perceived and the progress they had made since allowing the Fae to join the Council. Then, just as I was sure everyone in the gardens had almost nodded off, he dropped the bombshell.

"To ensure the ongoing harmony of relationships between the Inner City and the rest of England, the Assembly shall, from the end of the year, ask seven delegates from the unTalented to join our other allies in upholding the peace and providing protection for those who reside in this Realm. I trust you will all recognise the wisdom of this decision, which has been reached by unanimous agreement of the current assembly members."

Loud discussions broke out as the High Lord sat down. One by one, little bubbles of silence popped up as guests shielded their words with spells and charms, no doubt to discuss their reactions privately.

I watched the reactions at our own table closely. Stanley reached over and clasped Harrods arm.

"Good news eh? You'll be right pleased, I'd say." Harrod's face beamed in return. Clearly he hadn't expected this news. He turned to the Duke and Duchess Undridge and raised his glass for another toast.

A couple at a nearby table sniffed, scowled at each other, then stood up and walked out, followed by several shocked looks and some tittering from their dinner companions. Even I knew that would cost them politically.

Aware of the mixed feelings around us, conversation at the table was kept to other, less volatile topics—where Harrod was living, what Stanley and Bart had been up to, some minor issues the Duke had run into while managing his estate. As the men launched into a lively discussion about how best to ward off dark hound attacks on silkes, the Duchess turned to me.

"Ah, these men. Ever eager to talk of game and hunting. I imagine you'll meet tonight's announcement with some joy?"

"Yes, of course." I shot a glance around us to see if anyone was in earshot.

"Don't worry dear, no one can hear us." The Duchess made a small gesture towards her wand – she had warded us in a bubble of silence. "Your father worked hard for this. He would be so pleased to see that it's finally come to fruition."

"Thank you. It really is wonderful news for my kind," I said.

"Come now dear, you should be jumping for joy. I wouldn't blame you, it's been far too long coming and we do have a long way to go, but every step forwards is one less to take, yes?"

"Yes," I said carefully. "Until the assembly members start disappearing; until they ask for help or they oppose something the Talent lords have planned for them. Do you really think it will hold?"

"Ah, but the assembly isn't just Talented." The Duchess lifted a cautionary finger. "The Fae have long wondered when unTalented and half-skill would be included in the assembly. Once your people are sworn in, they will have powerful allies backing them up. That is why it has taken so long for the High Lord to gain consensus—this will be no token gesture, not at all."

"The High Lord didn't mention 'my people', only the unTalented." I smiled wryly. "It seems that, once again, it's my people who are caught in between—accepted by neither and hated by most."

"I think you'll be fine. The agreement really is designed to encompass the whole world outside our tiny city. And beside, the

half-bloods I've known over the years were an industrious bunch."
Duchess Columbine smiled at me. "Now, please do tell me how you
met Harrod. He's quite the lovely young man, I'm so pleased he's
found someone."

"He's found...? Oh, no! No, it's not like that. No, we're just
friends." My face was pinker than the wine I gulped down, thor-
oughly embarrassed at her assumption that Harrod and I were
dating. Casting around in my mind for anything else on earth to talk
about, I asked about her estate, and she happily chatted about their
lands and livestock while I tried to regain my composure.

Faske by the dozen emerged to serve the first of the delicacies—
the first course, tiny slices of pickled mandarin with lotus syrup. I
nibbled at the dish, taking note of the interactions around me. Many
of the silent pockets had dispersed and a more normal flow of chatter
drifted over the gardens. I couldn't see where Ave was sitting—that
was probably a good thing. As we ate, Harrod leaned close to speak
to me. Just before he spoke, someone came up to our table.

"Harrod!" High Master Abnett waited for Harrod to stand, then
clasped his arm in a familiar way. "Ah, this is your date? Beautiful
and famous." I blushed and stammered but he didn't give me the
chance to respond. "Your father was a true asset to our community,
Emmeline. We are so glad you've returned. You run a tea shop I hear?
Wonderful, wonderful. Now, I assume you're here for the same
reason Charles was always faffing about. You're to join the movement, of course! We'll find a position for you, my dear, nothing too
strenuous I assure you, but something important nonetheless. Now
Harrod, I just need a quick word, my friend..." Abnett dragged
Harrod off to another table where he descended on the guests in a
similar manner. Harrod gave me a pained look of apology as they left.

Much to my dismay, they moved on to another table out of sight
a few moments later. Columbine noticed my distress and placed a
gentle hand on my arm. "Now dear, you're among friends. It must
be terribly overwhelming to make your debut at a gala event, and

such an important one at that. No matter, we'll take good care of you."

Her words caused me some relief, until the next dish arrived. It looked like a white slug on a small biscuit, drizzled in a garishly red sauce. Columbine saw it and wrinkled her nose delicately.

Stanley caught me eyeing the plate and laughed. "Looks revolting, doesn't it? It's not so bad as all that, it's a moon fruit, something the Fae grow over *there*." I poked at the morsel and cut the end off. Soft, viscous liquid oozed out. Holding my breath and praying I wouldn't gag, I popped it in my mouth and swallowed without chewing.

Stanley clapped. "Brave girl. You're better than Harrod, he won't touch the things."

Levelling a flat expression at him for a moment, I then turned back to the Duchess who was watching our exchange with a smile. "You young ones. I can't say I'm as eager to try it myself." She set her cutlery down on the table and pushed her plate away. A faske popped up and immediately took it. Not feeling so bad for declining to eat more, I did the same and a few moments later, all the plates were gone. I noticed Stanley hadn't touched his moon fruit, either.

The next dish was a stuffed mushroom which was utterly delicious. By this stage my wine glass was empty and the chatter at our table flowed freely. Much of it wafted around me, but Harrod's friends did make an effort to include me often and by the time he returned to the table I felt easy in their presence.

"I think I've found where Opius is sitting," he said in a low voice. "We can't see him from here, but he's behind that woman over there, the one in the red."

The 'one in the red' was a woman in a garish dress who looked like she was trying to imitate a peacock. A feathered headpiece sat atop her hair and more splayed from her back, obscuring our view of anyone sitting in her path. "Dammit," I said, frustrated.

"You'll know him," Harrod said. "He's the only one here who

doesn't look healthy, though he's not nearly as bad as some of the accounts make out."

The skill of healers in the Inner City meant this would be rare indeed. *And yet, he will be the second Talent Lord I've met with a mysterious, incurable disease...*

I wondered, not for the first time, what was wrong with Jacoby. Perhaps it was contagious, and he had passed it on to Opius – or the reverse. Talent could cure nearly any disease, except a rare few that attacked both the body and the ability to use Talent itself. It could be a slow process but eventually, those with a disease like that would lose the ability to trace even the smallest of spells. I shuddered. Even with my meagre amount of power, losing it would affect every aspect of my life. For a full Talent? It would be unthinkable.

"I wonder if we could get her to move?" I mused, looking away from the feathered woman nervously. I was terrified that Opius would recognise me... or that I would recognise him.

"I doubt it. The only people I know at that table are ones I wouldn't normally be seen talking to. I don't want to draw attention."

"How good *are* you?" I asked. "Could you move something without anyone detecting that you'd done it?"

"Well... yes, I could. What are you thinking?"

All we had to do was get her to bend down or move over. I murmured this aloud and Harrod grasped what I was suggesting. His wand darted under the table and suddenly, the woman stood up, cursing.

"Oh, you clumsy pig!" she exclaimed to the man next to her. He paid her little heed—he seemed to be in a bit of a stupor. The commotion had drawn a few eyes so I didn't need to be overly shy about looking. She moved to the side, enough that I caught a glimpse of someone I recognised. My heart went cold.

"Do you see him?" Harrod asked in a low voice.

"The man with the bald head? That's Jacoby Priest."

"Who?"

"Jacoby Priest. Harrod, it must be a mistake, someone got the two mixed up." I clung to that small shred of hope even if my stomach twisted in fear. "He comes into my shop sometimes."

Harrod caught my arm, forcing my attention back to him. "Emma, I know every damn Lord in the Inner City, by name if not by face. There is no Jacoby Priest. *That's Opius.*"

I went cold. "The Guardians knew. Harrod, they showed me his face when we visited them in the Other, I just didn't want to believe it. Priest – *Opius* – comes into my shop *all the time.*" I felt the blood drain from my face and I started to tremble. "Maybe that's how he found his victims. Gods, what if this is all my fault?"

My stomach turned at the thought of this cretin stalking his victims from my shop. Before I could tear my eyes away, Opius looked up. When his eyes met mine, a smile spread across his face. He raised his glass as if to toast me from across the garden, then turned to speak to his companion. It was Ave.

Harrod put his hand on mine and squeezed it. In a low voice, he said "Now we know who he is we can stop him. I won't let him get near you again. I promise I'll keep you safe."

"Can we go?" I asked.

He nodded. Harrod said something to the others about taking a stroll before the next course arrived. We stood, and he guided me towards the rose gardens. We walked along a small rocky path, not smooth like the enchanted lawns. The smell of flowers was overwhelming and made my head feel light. When the uneven ground made me stumble, Harrod caught my arm to steady me. Perhaps the wine was a little stronger this side of the Wall.

We circled around back towards the manor, taking care to watch out for other wanderers. "Will leaving early cause you any trouble?" I murmured to Harrod.

"Not likely," he said. "We got through the important stuff. They'll probably think we went for a romp in the bluebells." He blushed when he realised what he'd said and stammered an apology. I couldn't help but laugh at that.

Just as we neared the end of the garden path, we heard talking. Harrod pulled me back into the bushes.

"Yes, of course. I understand how badly this news could affect one such as yourself. Terrible decision it was."

We couldn't make out the mumbled reply.

"Ah yes, of course. Very well then. Farewell Aveline. We shall call on you before the week is out."

I froze. Ave was right around the corner. Footsteps approached and I looked at Harrod in dismay. They reached the gravel path and, without a single other idea, I grabbed the back of his neck and pulled him into a kiss. I wrapped my arms around his neck, shielding both our faces. Harrod leaned into the kiss, pulling me closer to him. Our bodies pressed together and heat rushed through my body. After the sound of crunching gravel passed, I pulled back, trembling and gasping for air.

"Wow." Harrod blinked slowly. "Um, you're... really quick on your feet. Are you ok?"

I gave Harrod a shaky smile. "I thought we were done."

"Done? Oh!" Harrod tugged at his tie. "You mean—well no one knows we're looking for him, do they? Even if Aveline had seen us leaving, she couldn't have done anything about it."

"The first time I'm seen in Talented society in years and I suddenly up and leave without notice, right after seeing her with Opius?" I shook my head. "She might be a bitch but she's far from stupid. Who was she with, did you catch a look? It didn't sound like Opius."

"Ah... no. No, I didn't. I was a little busy."

I eyed him. "You know that was strictly business, right?"

"Business?"

"Yes. The business of saving our behinds. I know my good looks and girlish charm can be distracting, but keep your eyes on the game, Harrod." I turned away to hide my grin.

No need to let him know I was as flustered as he was. As frustrating as Harrod could be, the man was quite adorable when he was nervous. The way he stammered and blushed was, in its own way, quite charming. Now, if I could only keep us alive long enough to figure out what I wanted to do with that. Speaking of keeping us alive...

"Harrod, what you said at the table. I'm not your responsibility. I'm a grown woman, I do have a bit of talent and I make up for what I lack in tenacity and gumption." My voice softened. "Sometimes, you just can't keep another person safe. It has to be up to them to figure out how to do that... and sometimes, they don't."

Chapter Twenty-One

We left the manor without being seen, dodging a few small clusters of chatting nobles. Harrod had arranged for his driver to wait for us a few streets over so that he would be ready to go when we needed. Surely, there would be ramifications for Harrod. No doubt the whole damn guest list had noticed our early departure. I doubted he was right that it wouldn't be remarked upon; the Lords were such sticklers for propriety.

As we walked, fatigue set in. Lost sleep, high emotions and the stress of the evening had worn away the last vestige of whatever it was that had kept me going. Even Bee's enchantment had worn off—I no longer felt the easy grace and effortless movement she had bestowed on me for a time. The dim lighting in the street sparkled in the night, making it seem like Christmas. I dragged my feet and shivered, realising that outside the magical ambiance of the party, the night air was chill. Harrod wrapped an arm around my shoulders. He seemed no better than I was, yawning and leaning into me. Streetlights dotted the road, tall poles with lanterns atop, containing imbued gems that gave off an amber glow. Fog drifted in around our feet, making everything look hazy.

"How far is the car? My feet are killing me."

Harrod pointed to a side street and said Davoss, his driver, should be waiting there for us. We turned down the street. It was small and poorly lit... and empty.

"Wait, this isn't right. I must be more tired than I thought, this isn't supposed to be a dead end. Damned way-streets."

A sick feeling of deja-vu settled in my gut. I grabbed Harrod's arm and walked towards the brick building that closed off the street. As we approached it, the world tilted. Somehow, despite nothing moving, the street continued on... there was no dead end. Fear washed over me. Harrod stopped walking and shook his head.

"Harrod, we have to go back. It's a dream, we're in a dream." My voice shook and I felt my hands trembling on his arm.

"Ridiculous, it can't be." Nonetheless, Harrod darted an uncomfortable glance at the twisting we had just walked through. "We were walking, awake. He can't just take us; we have to be at least tired." He started back up the street, seemingly determined to go on.

"Tired... or a little tipsy? Fatigued after a long day, dancing, wine, and dinner?"

Harrod just kept walking, a stubborn look on his face. "I'm sure it's just..." He looked around. "Ah. I'm sorry, what were we talking about?"

"Harrod!" I shook his arm and he looked at me distractedly. "This is what he did to me. I was awake, walking, but so tired I could drop. Just like tonight. He's here, he has to be."

"Who's where?" Harrod spoke distractedly while he set off again up the street.

"Harrod, do you trust me?" I grabbed his shoulders and forced him to stop and look at me.

"Of course. Look, let's try that way." He pointed at an alley that had appeared out of nowhere.

I pulled him into a corner. Then, I slapped Harrod across the face. He started, flinching back and hitting his head against the wall behind him.

"What did you do that for?" He raised a hand to his face, giving me an injured look.

"I was hoping it'd wake you up!"

"What are you talking about? We're both perfectly awake, we just left the Gala. The car's just around the corner."

"Harrod, we've gone too far. We have to turn back."

Harrod started forwards again and I considered slapping him harder. I pulled him back behind me, trying to figure out what to do.

You can't save him a voice whispered in my head. *You have to run. He's caught, there's no way to get him out.*

Bullshit. I wouldn't leave him.

What if Opius comes for you again? What if he wins this time? You can always go back for Harrod.

No. Frantically I shook my head, desperation building.

Oh well. It might be easier this way anyway.

As the thought passed, the sound of it changed. I realised it wasn't a voice in my head, it was a voice in my ear... it sounded like Opius, but the words came from Harrod's mouth. I turned and my heart stopped when I saw what he held. He leaned back against the wall, examining the grail-knife with unfocused eyes. I slowly backed away, but the motion caught his eye.

"Emma, look what I found! It's the knife. I guess he didn't need it after all." Harrod twirled it between his fingers, caught it, and pointed it at me. I flinched.

"Harrod, put it down."

"What? No, then he'll come back for it. We need to hold on to it. Here, come and have a look—it's quite pretty when you see it up close." He gestured with the knife for me to come closer. I edged away instead.

"Harrod, *please*. Listen to me, just put the knife on the ground, and we can talk about it." I raised my hands, trying to calm him.

He looked at me, frowning. His hand gripped the knife a little tighter as he took a step towards me. I skittered back.

"Why do you want the knife?" His voice dropped to a threatening growl. "Why are you trying to take it from me?"

"I don't want it; I want you to put it down." I slowly raised my hands. "Harrod, we're caught in a dream. You *have* to listen to me."

"No. No, I don't think I'm going to give it to you. I know you want to use it on me." His face hardened. "If you had my power, you could be strong, respected. You want that, don't you?"

Tears pricked my eyes as I continued easing back. I didn't know how to fight this. I didn't know how to get myself out, let alone Harrod, if that was indeed him and not a dream image. He seemed to be completely under the spell and I had no doubt Opius had the skill to make Harrod's hand slip as soon as I was within arm's reach. I couldn't leave him—he was too powerful for Opius to pass up the opportunity—but I didn't know what to do.

"Come here, Emma." Harrod took a step towards me. "Come here. Now."

"No, Harrod. I'm so sorry. This is all my fault; I shouldn't have come with you. I'm sorry."

"Emma, what are you holding? Why is your wand out?"

My hands were still up in plain sight, empty. Opius had him convinced I was dangerous and I had no idea how to break the spell. A sob choked me. I turned and fled.

"Emma!" Harrod's voice screamed after me, sounding furious. I ran, darting between two buildings then taking another corner immediately after. I didn't know the Inner City well enough to find my way around, but I knew Opius was likely controlling the layout anyway. I could hear footsteps running behind me but I didn't turn to look.

I kept on, taking random corners and at one point, doubling around. Footsteps slapped on the pavement behind me, getting louder, then moving away, reappearing closer than before. Every now and then I'd hear Harrod call my name, looking for me. Sometimes it was in anger—others it sounded like he was lost and frightened. My chest heaved, gasps of air too strained to be quiet. I couldn't keep this up for much longer.

I found an open door leading into a small kitchen. Unsure if I was walking straight into a trap, I ducked inside. It was a room, dark but ordinary looking. I picked up a chair—if nothing else, I could use it to fend off Harrod, hopefully without hurting him too much. The tap-tap of shoes on cobblestones approached, slowly now. He knew he had me cornered.

I backed up behind the table.

"Oh, Emma. Must you be so terribly difficult?"

When he spoke I jerked in dismay. His voice was wrong, even more wrong than before. The man in front of me looked like Harrod, but it wasn't, I could see it in his eyes.

Opius.

"Come, now. Put the chair down. You'll hurt your friend." Harrod walked up to the doorway, filling it. He wasn't a tall man, but here, he seemed to have grown.

I tried to remind myself it was a dream, that what I saw wasn't real. "Why do you keep coming after me? Surely I'm not worth your effort."

"My dear, you are so *very* worth it. More than your little friend in fact. You see, it seems you have a very rare gift. A gift I very much need." Harrod sighed wistfully. "If I could take it another way, I would. I tried—I tried to leave the others alive, I did, but the power I gained only lasted such a short time. Just long enough to make me remember what it was like."

Harrod—or, Opius in Harrod's body—approached the table. Warily, I edged back and to the side, keeping it between us. I'd caught my breath a little—if I could circle round and dash out the door, I might be able to run for a little while longer. I wasn't sure what good that would do, though.

"I'm dying, Emma. Me. I was one of the most powerful Talents in the City, perhaps even in the world. I helped to bring about the agreements, I fought for equality, I spent ten years, *ten years* in outer London, helping the mortals. I don't deserve to die."

"Why are you telling me this?"

"So that you understand. So you know how very sorry I am, so you know I had no choice." Harrod edged around the left and I let him, keeping the balance to one side.

"Bullshit. There's always a choice." *That's it, slowly. Don't make him go back towards the door.*

"Emma, if I was here..." Harrod lifted his eyes to mine, a cold, piercing gaze that prickled my skin. "Would you kill me to save yourself?"

"You're attacking me and holding my friend hostage. If I killed you, it would be self-defense," I growled. "Anything else would be murder. There is *no* justification for that."

"Oh, child. I suppose I would have said the same when I was young. It's only when you stare death in the face that you realise how much you value life."

Just a little more...

I had to keep him talking, keep him distracted. "I've seen death, Opius. He came for someone I love. I know his face; I've stared into it. He left me behind, but it doesn't change anything."

Harrod stood back and sighed. "I should let you know; I was going to let this one live. I'm not against taking him if I have to. With his power, I can simply come for you directly."

Rage filled me and with it, something slid over my skin. As the feeling passed, everything shifted a little. We were still in a kitchen but it was now three times the size, and glow lamps suffused the space with light. A faske sat in the corner balled up as small as he could. The door I'd been about to run for was a solid wall—the actual doorway was several feet to one side. I shook my head, confused.

"You won't let him live, you're too power hungry," I said, trying to stall him until I figured out where we really were.

"Power? No dear." He lifted the knife again, tipping its point toward me. "Just life. Life is enough for me now, but I won't settle for less. I tasted your gift, you know. It stopped the disease in its tracks. Only for a few days, but how glorious that was. I could feel it pull back, feel the strength in my limbs, the magic flow through me again. I won't give that up, not for anyone."

As he spoke I shifted my body, hiding my right hand from his view. I worked my wand free with as little movement as possible. With no idea if my plan had any chance of working, I traced the fastest spell I knew and threw it at him. A ball of light exploded in Harrod's face. It wasn't bright enough to blind him, but it took him by surprise. It also told me something, something very important. *I wasn't dreaming anymore.*

Harrod lunged and I bolted. Anticipating my move, he shoved at the table and it clipped my hip bone, making me fold over in pain. Still hunched, I clumsily threw a chair at him and hobbled to the door. I pulled it closed just as he slammed against it. A quick spell to lock it and I waited, hoping. To my relief, he battered the door but couldn't get through. Opius could control Harrod's body, his voice, but tapping into his magic was harder.

But perhaps not impossible. I remembered the strange slipping sensation that had felt just like Harrod and Deirdre's attempts to heal on that day so long ago.

Very well. A shiver ran through me and I froze as Opius' voice bounced through my head. *I shall take him myself.*

The noises at the door stopped and a feeling of dread filled me. I ran for the door and traced a spell, throwing it back open in time to see Harrod raise the knife, its point directed at his torso. He turned his head to look at me with sad eyes.

I threw myself at Harrod and we fell to the ground. The knife dropped and he twisted away to grab it. I kicked it, and the knife went skidding across the floor. Harrod threw his fist and it connected with my face. My head rang in pain. He rolled on top of me, pinning me down, then climbed over me towards the knife. I reached out, found the leg of the chair, and pulled it down on top of him. The distraction was enough to let me push him off me, kicking him in the face as I scrambled for the knife. Grabbing it, I hurled it towards the door. I pointed my wand and cast a desperate spell, sending it flying off into the distance. Harrod jumped to his feet and took off after it, and I sprinted after him.

He skidded to a halt just past the doorway. When I saw what stopped him, a sob of relief escaped.

Barg stood in the middle of the street, holding the knife. He looked at it in confusion. Harrod plunged forwards and I screamed, "Run!"

Barg took a bewildered look at the Talent running for him and took off. The hobgoblin practically flew along the street, then bounded up a wall and across a rooftop. Harrod raced after him but within seconds, Barg had disappeared.

While Harrod was distracted chasing after the knife, I slipped down a side street to catch my breath. I was back in the real world now—it had happened in the house when the room changed, I was sure of it. My gift thrummed inside of me. I remembered the feeling vaguely, from my childhood. It felt familiar and safe, but I wasn't sure how to use it yet. I didn't know how to snap Harrod out of the dream. I could stay and fight, but that could end up in both of us getting hurt. I *had* to take out Opius... somehow.

The muted sounds of music and revelry floated through the air. If the Gala ended before I found Opius, the streets would be flooded with high-ranking Talents. Despite the complete lack of response to Opius's actions so far, attacking someone like Harrod would cause an uproar. The gods only knew what he'd be willing to do to save himself.

Thinking hard, I tried to reason out Opius's location. If I could hear the celebrations, we probably hadn't gone far. Stuck in a dream state, we could have been running in circles the whole time. That meant he would probably be close by...

I started in the direction Barg and Harrod had gone, moving as fast as I dared without being seen. The lack of life around me added an extra layer of unease. Would Barg head for the Wall, or the centre of the Inner City? Stumped, I paused to get my bearings. I could see the Wall behind me, lit along the upper edge with decorative globes of light. They hadn't headed for the Wall then. Shaking my head and wishing I had something to go on, I began to hurry ahead when I heard a shout. It sounded like Harrod, and it was coming from behind me.

As I ran, I kept to the shadows, stepping lightly on the cobbles and doing my best to stay quiet.

"Give me the knife!" That was definitely Harrod, and it wasn't far off.

I veered left and took a sharp turn, then skidded to a halt as someone disappeared into a doorway just ahead. Torn, I looked in the direction of the yell I'd heard. I didn't know how far away they were, and I probably couldn't help them anyway. After a deep breath, I crept up to the door and placed my hand on it. It swung open smoothly.

Inside, the house was cloaked in silence, shadows stretching across the room. Perhaps he'd left through another exit? No. There was the slightest sound from above me, shifting weight on old floorboards. Wand out in front of me, I crept up the stairs, with a spell on my lips. I hesitated near the top.

"Don't stop. Come out where I can see you."

He spoke gently, and I remembered that I'd first known the man as Jacoby Priest, the quiet, kind Talent that visited my shop. That made me angry. I closed my eyes, concentrating on the direction of his voice. Tracing a spell of distraction, I slipped into the room. Opius laughed at me, not at all affected by my meagre attempt at magic. He sat on a chair by the window, a stone golem standing motionless by his side.

"You tiny thing. So weak." His wands barely twitched. I fell to the ground, agony tearing through every limb in my body. My voice dissolved in my throat as I tried to scream, air ripping past my throat and creating nothing but silence. I heaved a breath in, squeezing and eyes shut and—*pop*. The pain was gone like a rope that had unravelled, slipping harmlessly to the floor. Tiny gasps escaped from my chest. I turned my eyes towards Opius, holding the power I'd used. Power that terrified him. Power that he lusted for.

The golem's arm reached out and pulled Opius into a standing position. He flicked his wand at me again, but the spell slipped off me.

Again. Again. Each attempt made his eyes grow bigger, his breath come faster. He couldn't touch me. His next spell was aimed a little to the side, but I wasn't smart enough to realise why.

A small box struck my side. It hurt badly and I crumpled over in pain. Clearly, I hadn't quite thought this through. I ducked as a lamp was hurled at my head, then dived to the side as the floor cracked underneath me.

This has to end, fast. Years of tussles with my sisters had taught me there was one thing I could always count on—Talents, powerful ones, used magic to the exclusion of all else. They relied on it so much it didn't even occur to them that others didn't.

I dodged another piece of furniture, this time moving so I was closer to him. Taking note of the distance, I dropped to the ground as a footstool flew over my head. When a curtain ripped off its rails and twisted towards me, I launched myself at him.

We connected, Opius crashing into the wall behind him. He was old, and his body ravaged by disease. Something crunched under the weight of my forearm and I hoped it was his neck—no such luck. He struggled under my weight and his wand jabbed my side as he tried to wield it. I used mine, a small, simple spell of motion. He cast his spell at the same time. The two spells connected, ricocheted off each other. I flew back, crashing into the wall across the room with a thunderous sound. I looked up, dazed by my fall, to see the hole where the window had been.

I crawled over, dust floating through air lit by a street globe. I looked out over the cobblestones to find Opius lying on them, body broken and twisted. Moonlight lit the scene and sparkled on the pool of blood that slowly spread around him.

Coughing, I made my way downstairs. I waited there, watching. Nothing. No rise and fall of the chest, no movement at all. I stepped into the street to check properly, but ducked back again when I heard a slow, hollow scrape. The golem, now missing a leg and a big piece of its head, shuffled over to Opius and awkwardly picked him up. He started walking down the street with the Talent Lord, away from me. If Opius had died, the golem would have disappeared. How had he survived a fall like that? I started after them.

I'd only gone a short way when a big, solid arm caught me up. I screamed, voice muffled in a rough, leathery chest and pounded my hands at it.

"Lady! Lady, iss Gibble. Lady, Gibble iss here to help."

I stopped at the familiar voice, then collapsed into his arms, letting him hold me as I cried.

"Lady, we mussst go. People. People come."

"Harrod..."

"Gibble find." The boggart sniffed the air, then scooped me up over his shoulder. He took off at a run. Despite his speed, I was barely jostled. Just two streets on, he stopped and placed me back on the ground, frowning. Then, he looked up.

"What issss little man on roof for?" A face peered over the top of the building we looked up at.

"Hello, Lady! Master Gibble! Barg is at your services!"

"Where's Harrod?" I called up to him.

"Ah. Lady, I ran! I did not know why, but I ran! Little man chased me and tried to follow. Barg is good climber! Man is not. He did climb though. Lady? Man must have used up all his, his...

waking? He is having sleep." His voice dropped to a whisper that was somehow as loud as his yell. "Lady? Man is very noisy sleeper."

Gibble hoisted me up to the rooftop. I just managed to grab on and pull myself up with Barg's help. He was small but stronger than he looked. Harrod was near the edge of the roof, unconscious and breathing loudly past an oddly twisted neck. Rushing to him, I lifted his head and his breath quietened.

"What happened? Was he hurt?"

"No, Lady! Man was chasing. Man is Talent, but man did not use. Barg thought maybe it was a game! Barg loves games! So I ran and did not let man catch the prize, but Barg thinks games are not fun after you win. Barg let man get close sometimes. Then, man just went to sleep. Children have sleep after games, yes? Maybe man decided it was a good idea."

"How long ago Barg?" Dread formed in the pit of my stomach.

"Lady, not very long at all. Moon has barely moved. Barg was going to stay and watch, in case he wanted to play again."

"Gibble?" I leaned over the side of the rooftop to call down to him. "We need to get Harrod down. Can you catch him?"

Gibble nodded. After a quick conversation with Barg, I rolled Harrod's limp body to the edge of the rooftop. Saying a quick prayer to whatever the hell kind of Gods covered a situation like this, I dropped him off. Gibble caught him easily and I sighed with relief.

Once I was down myself we made our way back to Harrod's. We arrived to bedlam—Barg had gone ahead to summon Deirdre and they had arrived before us. Bee was there, which I hadn't expected. Martin was pacing across the room, out of his mind with worry. When we came through the door, he rushed over, helping Gibble to lie Harrod down on the floor. Deirdre bent over to examine him and I gave the short version of what happened—that Opius had been controlling Harrod when I knocked him out. She waved her wand over him, concentrating, then sat back and shook her head.

"This kind of magic hasn't been around for a very long time. I could try to break him free, but I don't know what that would do."

Martin cursed and thumped the wall beside him. He didn't look at me, but I knew what he was thinking.

"It's my fault," I said, voice shaking with fatigue and emotion.

"You did what you could." Martin refused to look at me. Bee placed a soothing hand on his shoulder but he shook it off.

"I need to get out of this dress. Bee?"

I turned and walked out. When we got upstairs, I started ripping off the dress as fast as I could. Bee just watched, disapproving.

"I like that one," she said.

"He's gorgeous, you're Fae. Of *course* you like him."

She spread her hands with elegant nonchalance. "I cannot tell a lie, you know that."

"I'm sure you can twist your words with the best of them."

"I don't like to deceive those I care for." Red lips were pursed disapprovingly.

"Then figure something out!" I immediately regretted the irritation in my voice. This wasn't her problem.

"Oh child," Bee said. "This isn't your fault. You are the one who needs to fix it, but you cannot see the greater plan. Trust. I will make your excuses while you steal away to rescue the dragon."

Bloody Fae and their mangled expressions. Still, I sighed in relief. It was every bit my fault, I knew that, but Bee had my back. She'd distract the others while I slipped out. Now dressed in the clothes I'd arrived in, I gave Bee one last tremulous smile. Then, I climbed out the window.

Chapter Twenty-Two

B arg met me down the end of the street as we'd discussed on the rooftop. I felt bad for sneaking off, but I knew Gibble and Martin would both insist on coming and I couldn't risk any more of my friends. He handed me the knife, and I slipped it through my belt.

"Did you find out where it is?" I asked in a low voice.

"Yes, Lady!" He saluted me proudly.

"Shh! Keep it down."

"Yes, La—*yes, Lady*."

"That's better. Off we go then." I turned to walk, then stopped and looked back as I realised he wasn't following.

Barg stood there, toeing the ground and looking away.

"Barg?"

"Lady, Barg still owes Gibble much debt..."

"He told me that was cleared." I frowned. He couldn't lie, neither could Gibble. I waited in silence for a moment, watching him fidget. Barg heaved a sigh.

"Well, the *first* debt is cleared. When Gibble was away, Barg might have used his name in a tiny little wager." He lifted big, mournful eyes. "Barg might have lost. Barg is in Gibble's debt, again."

"That doesn't matter. By not telling, you're paying him back, I promise." He looked unconvinced. "Fine. If you leave me, I'll go anyway and I'll probably get killed. Then you won't have the chance to tell him you saved me."

Barg's eyes widened in horror as he contemplated the outcome of my death, and having to tell Gibble he'd known what I was doing. His wide mouth opened, closed, then opened again. Finally, his shoulders sagged. He set off down the street, muttering about boggarts preferred methods of killing wayward hobgoblins.

We passed back into the Inner City, Barg using some kind of dust from the Other to put the guards at the gate into a deep sleep. It seemed the Gala had come to an end—the barren streets were now dotted with people walking or driving home, dressed in all their splendour. We stayed to the shadows and managed to get to our destination unseen.

"Can you get me in?" I asked. The mansion was huge and opulent, befitting a man with the station Opius claimed to have held.

"Ye—" Barg stopped, then started again in a whisper. "Yes, Lady! The dust of hiding things will... it will make you a hidden thing. It is goodly named, unlike the syrup of candlescent. That made Barg smell like the bottom end of a bearded sorn't. It—"

"Barg. Please." I groaned internally, wondering if I'd made the right choice in bringing him with me.

He stopped talking and pulled out a small bag. Stroking it and mumbling something about the cost, he opened it and poured something very carefully into his hand. Without warning, he blew a handful of what felt like fine dirt in my face. It tickled my nose, making me sneeze. When it settled, I looked down. I wasn't quite invisible, but I had a transparent look and blended into shadows.

"That will keep Lady from setting off magical traps. You can still be seen, Lady, so Lady be very, very careful or Lady be getting Barg into Very Big Trouble."

Of course—if I got killed, *Barg* would be in trouble. I snorted, then set off to find a way into the house. It didn't take long. The Talented wardings would keep out the majority of intruders so security tended to be lax inside the City itself. The only things that could sneak through would need Fae help. Because they so very rarely worked with humans, it was a safe bet that if they were involved, you had no chance of survival anyway.

I climbed through an open window and crossed the kitchen. After making a brief circuit of the bottom floor to find it empty I crept upstairs, knife gripped in one hand. Finally, I found the right room. Small noises came from the room—strained, raspy breathing and a low crooning. I slid around the corner and was shocked at what I found.

Opius was tucked up in bed, blankets to his chin. His skin was an unhealthy shade of grey, and inside the room, his breathing sounded worse. Beside him sat the stone golem, stroking his head. It was easy to believe any breath would be his last. I had to do this—I hoped that his death would release Harrod from the dream, but I couldn't be sure. There was a small chance that he'd be sucked into the After along with Opius if his grip was strong enough.

The knife was my security against that. Using it would absorb the last of the power Opius used to control dreams, pulling it away from him and forcing him to release his grip on Harrod. I would have to be careful; I needed Opius to lose his Talent before he took his last breath.

I stepped forward into the room and the golem turned its head to me. It couldn't attack me; golems were formed according to certain conditions that prevented that, otherwise the entire Inner City would be overrun by giant golems with a penchant for knocking heads together.

It attacked me. Everything went black.

~

I woke lying in bed. Well, *a* bed. It wasn't mine and I didn't know whose it was. Grey walls and a white ceiling surrounded me. The room was empty, except for me and the single bed I lay in. How did I get here? Where *was* here?

I remembered seeing Opius, then... nothing. Cautiously, I sat up. My body ached and felt oddly out of proportion for a moment, then everything righted. A pain pierced my head and I touched it gently, feeling a large bump that I didn't remember getting. It was tender from my hairline down to my cheekbone and I had a feeling it would look as bad as it felt.

My feet met a cold linoleum floor, and I stood gingerly, looking down at the hospital gown I wore. I shook my head in confusion, pain making me regret it immediately. I needed to get out of here... where was the door?

Right in front of me. It hadn't been there a moment ago; I was certain of it. Gingerly, I padded over in bare feet and opened it to peek outside. Instead of the hallway I'd expected, the door led into a stone room. It looked like a child's nursery, with a small bed and some toys scattered about. Sunlight streamed in through a large window, warm on my skin. Across the room, a small boy sat atop a toy horse, talking to something in his hand. He didn't notice me watching.

"Now Jones, Father says we mustn't dawdle. The new tutor starts today and we must show our best selves. I've been practising my Talent, watch."

He pulled out a small wand and flicked it in the air. Nothing happened. He tried again and this time, a tiny ball of light appeared. It was one of the first spells taught to a young Talent. This boy was strong; despite the brightness of the day, his globe was blinding. He paid me no heed as I edged around him towards the door, as if he didn't even know I was there. I fled the strange room and its inhabitant through another door, almost tripping on a crack in the floor on the way.

Somehow, I'd become trapped in Opius's dream. His gift had

flared as his body failed, catching me and drawing me in. Vague memories of being attacked by the golem lurked in my mind. Was I lying unconscious on the floor? What would the golem do with my body?

Shuddering, I turned my thoughts back to the immediate problem. I didn't know enough about dreamweaving to say for sure, but I could guess that being here when he died was probably not ideal. Escaping would just be a matter of embracing my gift and... *wait, what about Harrod?*

If Opius was this close to death, I might not have time to use the knife. I'd somehow undone the damage the Fae had caused to Harrod – could I undo Opius's magic, too? Harrod must be here somewhere. If I could find him, I might be able to bring him out of the dream with me.

With no idea how this dream world really worked, unsure if I could use my gift intentionally, going after Harrod could be risking my life on a hunch. Harrod might not be here. Even if he was, I might not be able to save him. What were the chances of a weak half-blood being able to rescue a Talent so much stronger than me? I stepped through the door. Giving up wasn't an option, not if I had even the slimmest chance of saving Harrod. A low rumble shook the building, and a shower of crumbled stone drifted down from above. Dread settled in the pit of my stomach.

The next room held a study. The boy again, now at a desk and writing furiously. His free hand darted into a pocket, fumbling at something, then returned to the desk. A moment later, the hand was in the pocket again and I saw a tiny white rat poke its head out to sniff the air. The boy quickly put his hand back to the desk.

Crack!

A thin stick slapped down across his knuckles. I started. A thin, pallid looking man in blue livery had appeared.

"You will concentrate, Mikael. If I see that rodent again I shall drown it like the last one."

The boy looked stricken for a moment. I edged towards the next door. Before I turned away to open it, the boy turned to me.

"It doesn't matter if he kills it again." His eyes bored into me. "I'll die soon anyway, won't I?"

Something tickled my shoulder. It was another crack in the ceiling, wide enough for the plaster to trickle down from the gap it created. I turned back to say something to the boy and jumped when I realised he was now standing right next to me.

"Why won't you save me?" My skin prickled as the serious boy with the dark eyes returned to his seat. His instructor hadn't seemed to notice that he'd even moved.

Unnerved, I ducked through the next door. Room after room, each one with a different scene being acted out. The boy was always there, at different ages. He grieved over the death of a beloved horse. He found the rat, Jones. He took his first class. He met with an old woman, a Talented Evaluator who told him he had the capacity to be the most powerful Talent in centuries. He met with a Talent healer, who sadly shook her head while delivering bad news.

I saw him as a teenager, crying as he struggled to stand. I saw the bright, vibrant light globes he produced as a child and moments later, the dim, weak ones he made as an adult. I watched Mikael Opius go through life, the bright promise of an extraordinary childhood torn away by an incurable illness. I saw the shame and disappointment of once proud parents, the cruelty of tutors who came expecting a prodigy and found something else. I saw how he was taught that power meant respect, that weakness was a failure of character. I watched as he fought for equality, then was ostracised by his few remaining friends for it and ridiculed for his inability by those he tried to help.

I didn't forgive Opius. I couldn't, he killed my friends; but I started to understand him.

Another door, but no childhood memories this time. Instead, a long corridor stretched out on either side. Cobwebs drifted down from the ceiling and the slate floor was gritty. No doors. Which way did I need to go?

I slapped the wall beside me in a bout of frustration. The corridor stretched out in both directions with no end. Running around blindly wouldn't just waste precious time, it could be downright dangerous. I'd accomplish nothing that way. I needed a plan, a way to navigate a world that had no consistency and defied the laws of physics.

Closing my eyes, I tried to calm down and focus, tried to think of a way to navigate this world made of dreams and inconsistencies. When I opened them a moment later, I staggered back in surprise.

Instead of the never-ending hallway, I was in a large, opulent room. Tapestries decorated the walls, showing many of the scenes I'd passed earlier, and a window looked out into a dusky sky. The room was dominated by a round table surrounded by empty chairs. There was a map covering the table showing a rough layout of a castle. It was dotted with tiny figurines—like chess pawns, but with faces carved on the tiny nubs. Careful not to touch anything, I circled around to see each one.

I found my own first. A white pawn with my face, sitting on a circular room on the map labelled 'War Room'. Harrod's figurine was in the dungeon. That didn't inspire confidence. Opius was in the Ivory Tower. The guy had delusions about his own importance, so why not? Something skittered across the page, then stopped next to my own piece. It was a fourth pawn, smaller than the others. Without thinking, I picked it up. It had a tiny rat face carved into it. I frowned, then carefully placed it back on the map.

Examining it more closely, I used my finger to trace a line from me to Harrod. Then, I did it again. The second time, the route was different. The map wasn't constant. In fact, everything about the map had changed. I hadn't seen the shift, but the colours were now washed out, the edges tattered. I darted a glance around the room to see a fine layer of dust coating everything. The rich tapestries that had hung on the wall were now rotting away and some of the chairs were missing, one upturned and missing a leg. That wasn't good.

If the map layout was changing, what use was it? I refused to believe it wasn't here for a reason. I'd needed it, and it had appeared, so why would that happen if it couldn't help in some way?

This was a dream and the rules of real life were different. Like the Otherworld, things were different depending on perception and need. Like the Otherworld...

I thought for a moment, then looked at the layout of the war room. The rat piece was in the corner, behind me. My mouth twisted into a grin when I turned to find a live, white rat.

~

He skittered into my hand when I leaned down and called him. Holding the rat up to my face, I looked into its little dark eyes.

"Ok Ratty, this is how we're gonna roll. You've been here a long time, right?"

The rat watched me. He didn't just look at me; he *watched* me.

"I need to find my friend. He's here."

I set the rat on the table and pointed to Harrod's likeness. The rat ran across the map to Harrod, then back to the room we were in. Then, he ran to Opius.

"He's dying."

Squeak. He still sat next to Opius.

"Do you understand that? He's going to die, and if he does, bad things will happen."

Squeak. A little more insistent this time.

"Fine. But Harrod first, OK? I need to get him out, then I'll try —I'll *try*—to get Opius out. No promises; if we run out of time, I'm leaving without him." How does one effectively bargain with a rat?

A pause. *Squeak.* Ratty ran back over to Harrod's place on the map, chirped again then dashed up my arm. Hoping beyond hope this would work, I headed for the door. This time, it opened into a different corridor, one with several doors. The white rat darted down to the ground, then across the hallway and up a little. It stopped twice to sniff the air, then settled in front of a large wooden door, licking its paws. I followed and placed a hand on the door. I took a breath and pushed.

It opened into a spiral stairwell winding down a circular tower. The balustrade was broken and bent, offering no support and once the door behind us swung closed, it was dark enough to make seeing difficult. Would magic work here?

Of course it would. I chided myself for being so fearful, then traced a globe of light, one of the few spells I could work without a wand. It was dark enough that even my weak globe seemed to light it well, if only for a short distance ahead. I let out a breath I hadn't realised I was holding.

My rodent guide led me down into the dark stairwell. Dungeons, I assumed, were generally located in a downward direction. The steps were uneven and crumbling at the corners, slowing my progress and almost causing me to fall more than once. We passed more doors. Just as we neared the next one, I stepped on a loose rock and went tumbling down, the little light globe bobbing as it followed. Arms over my head, I screamed as my body bounced down the stairs, smacking limbs and head on sharp stone corners.

Instead of slowing, I picked up speed. I panicked, knowing that if I rolled just the wrong way, I'd be over the edge and into the black darkness below. My foot caught on a bit of old balustrade jutting up from the side. It slowed me, but I tipped toward the edge. Heart stopping, I twisted myself towards the wall, and somehow managed to roll that way. Finally, I came to a stop, battered and bruised.

Crying in fear and pain, I leaned against the wall. I felt my limbs, prodded my face. Nothing felt broken as far as I could tell, but one foot was sore enough to make me whimper when I tried to stand on it. Using the wall for support I stood, balancing on my good foot. The effort made me pant, dank air filling my lungs. I looked around and found the white rat staring at me unsympathetically. I tried the foot again. This time, it held up a little better. I could have sworn rat-face raised an invisible eyebrow at me.

I hobbled down a few more stairs then, thankfully, through the door indicated by my whiskered guide. It led to a tiny outcropping attached to a bridge. The bridge—if you could call it that—was frail and narrow. It and stretched across a yawning chasm of nothingness.

"This isn't like any dungeon I've seen," But then, this wasn't a real dungeon – it was the dream of a man whose sanity had collapsed long ago.

As I stepped forward I felt the wind. It whipped through the void, buffered only by the shelter of the doorway I stood in. I backed up, but the door I'd passed through was now closed behind me. I tried it, more a reflex than any conscious thought. It was, of course, locked.

I had nowhere to go but across.

CHAPTER TWENTY-THREE

I gripped the railings on either side of the rickety bridge. It wasn't so much a fear of heights as it was a sensible respect. Traversing a broken down bridge, over an abyss, inside the head of a madman? Not sensible.

I didn't seem to have much choice, though. I tentatively placed my sore foot onto the wooden structure. The rough surface made me wish I had shoes on. I took another step. So far, so good. The bridge didn't shake, collapse or turn into a giant snake, so I kept going. I had to lean forwards against the gusty winds, one hand on the railing to support my injured foot. My light globe bobbed beside me, throwing shadows out into the nothing. By the time I reached the centre of the bridge I was moving a little faster.

Snap! The railing I held onto gave way, taking me with it. I toppled over the side of the bridge, my body yanked again as my descent was halted. The railing I gripped hadn't come all the way off. Instead, it dangled from a splintered post a short distance above me. On top of the leaning post sat the rat, calmly waiting to see what I'd do.

I couldn't do much. A rough wooden pole, barely attached, was all that kept me from certain death. Suddenly there was a wrenching sound. A portion of the bridge tore away, tearing one end from the other. The structure lurched sideways and I was jolted along with it, screaming in terror. My hand slipped a few inches along the railing. Splinters dug into my hands and my arms ached. I spasmed and nearly let go as something ran over my hand. It was the rat. He stopped and sat on the rail just above where I gripped it and twitched his nose at me.

"Lend me a hand?" I gasped.

He bit me. Piercing pain shot through my hand and I felt the only solid thing I could touch slip. Even holding on with everything I had, pulling every bit of reserve I had, my hand slid off the end of the railing. I fell.

I landed with a thud on a concrete floor, just a few feet below.

A rumble above and this time, instead of stone dust, pebbles rained down on me. I clambered back to my feet. I wasn't hurt—at least, not much more than I had been before my fall—and the bridge had vanished. Shaking but determined, I looked around for the rat. He sat in front of me with a patient expression, one paw rubbing an ear.

"What the hell? You didn't have to bite me."

Squeak. He ran over and licked one of my toes. An apology? He'd have to do better than that. He skittered off and I followed at my own limping pace. He didn't go too far ahead, occasionally turning back to chitter at me for my slow progress. We followed a wall that ran in a curved line to the left. It then turned sharply right and ahead, a huge stone arch built into it. The wall reached far enough above that there was no visible ceiling, just more darkness. Ratty waited for me at the entrance.

I stepped through and he ran up my leg and over the hospital gown. Once he was perched on my shoulder, he nestled in and waited for me to proceed.

We were in a cavernous room, shaped like a dome. A well-made but slightly rusted sword sat beside the archway and I picked it up. Things here had a purpose—I wasn't going to leave a weapon lying around for someone else to use. Across from us, a portcullis locked off another large entrance to the room, making it look like a gladiator pit. As soon as I noticed it, the iron gate rattled and began to rise. A quick check behind me revealed the archway we'd entered through had disappeared. Well then. I raised the sword in what I hoped looked like a battle stance and prepared for whatever was about to come through the gate. If only I had something other to wear than a cotton gown. A weight pressed down on me and I looked down to see a suit of chain mail had appeared in place of the hospital garb. That was handy.

"Oh, for crying out loud. No. No! *Damn you Opius.*" I yelled at the world around me. The words echoed in the chambers, bouncing back to me in a voice that didn't sound like mine.

My sweaty hands gripped the sword tightly as I prayed that whatever dumb luck had kept me alive so far held up. I didn't think there was much chance of it. Before me, snorting and shaking its head, was a dragon.

The first and only time I'd seen a dragon was on a trip to Antarctica with my father. A white scaled mother and child had flown over, then settled on a glacier to gnaw on an old penguin carcass.

If you've never actually seen a dragon, you can't accurately imagine it. They're not just huge. They're not just terrifying. They make your mind spin and your knees give way, they look into your soul and rip it apart.

Dragons are sentient, but not in the way we are. Nothing about them makes sense—their motives, their strange honour code, or their ability to fly with such aerodynamically unsound bodies.

This dragon was smaller than the ones I'd seen as a child. It was tiny. And by tiny, I mean it was about the size of a double-decker bus. I backed up until I hit the wall, sword out in front of me in a way I hope looked threatening, or at least indigestible. The rat nudged my ear lobe.

"Yeah buddy, he's big. I can take him, though… right?"

He let out a drawn-out squeak, like a sigh.

I mentally searched through my arsenal of spells, but there was nothing useful I could do without my wand. The rat squeaked in my ear. He sounded quite frantic. I didn't blame him. The dragon approached me, snorting warm air through oversized nostrils. It bared its teeth and a low growl rumbled through the cavern. I edged to the side, trying to back away from him.

The dragon's big body swayed to and fro, moving its weight from one giant foot to the other. Chain clinked and I noticed a length of it running along the floor. He was chained up. Well, any good guard beast is worth holding on to. The dragon pulled away from me and my heart dropped back to less than lethal speed.

He pounced. I flew backwards onto the floor, skull smacking on the packed dirt. My head exploded in pain and spots appeared in front of me. I curled into a ball, wrapping my arms around my head. The dragon roared, then swiped at me with a giant claw. It clipped my shoulder, sending me rolling to the side. I scrambled back on all fours to grab the sword and pressed my back against the wall again.

The dragon raised another paw but I was better prepared this time and rolled under it. I fumbled, landing on my side to my feet, sword back at the ready. I edged to the side, closer to the only opening in the room. He noticed my movement, and giant jaws snapped at me.

Fear got the better of me. I ran. Darting for the portcullis, I left the safety of the wall in the hope I could beat the monster to the opening. A claw slapped me to the ground, tumbling me over onto my back. The dragon stood over me and let out a screech. As it raised its head and exposed its neck, I brought the sword up. Needle sharp pain shot through my earlobe and I flinched, jerking the sword to the side as the beast swooped its head down and I missed my chance. That bastard rat had bitten me again.

The snarling dragon looked down at me. When our eyes met, an icy shock went through me. It wasn't the soul-shattering feeling of looking into the heart of a dragon. It was one of recognition. The dragon's eyes were wrong. Instead of swirling, opalescent pools, they were... human. Human eyes in a dragon.

When I realised what had nearly happened, I dropped the sword. Tears filled my eyes and I sucked in ragged gasps of air. The dragon twitched its head, confused. I could see him fighting, see him trying to work out what was wrong. He let out another screech, spreading out huge, leathery wings and gnashed his teeth at me again. I needed to make him see.

Mind racing, I dodged another attack. As he lifted his enormous head, I spied the metal collar circling his neck. The next time his head swung down, I grabbed the chain hanging from it and was wrenched into the air as he yanked away. The dragon swung his head, trying to throw me off as I clung to him. I used the momentum to climb the chain and grabbed on to the plates of his back. Gripping the collar to keep me steady, I threw one leg over his neck. Guided only by instinct, I placed a hand on his neck and pushed. I pushed my power into him, forcing it through scales, muscles, tendons. I funneled it into the massive beast, using every drop of strength I had.

The dragon stilled.

He lay on the ground, spent. I climbed off his neck, sliding down and landing on my good foot. My legs shook from exhaustion as I hobbled around to see his face. He looked at me, eyes filled with fear and confusion.

"Harrod?"

The dragon lifted his head just a little. He gave a single, small nod.

"Oh, Harrod. What has he done to you? Are you... I don't even know what to ask. I'll get you out of here, I promise. You'll be ok."

I placed a hand against the giant face and knew his anguish. He was still trapped. I'd used everything I had and though I'd broken part of the spell, we were still here. Another tremor made me lose my balance and I put my hand out to steady myself on the dragon. Ratty appeared, sitting on Harrod's face. A giant eye rolled over to look at my tour guide.

"Ok, Rat, how do I free him?"

The rat launched himself off the dragon and onto the floor. He ran to the sword.

"What? I can't kill him, he's my friend! What if it goes wrong?"

Shooting me a withering glare, he squeaked and ran back to the dragon—to Harrod. He climbed the chain, then sat on the collar. Looking more closely, I saw a kind of mechanism holding it closed. Oh, right. He didn't want me to kill the dragon, but free it. I picked up the sword and a moment later, had pried off the collar and chain. Rat sat atop Harrod's neck where I'd been a short time before. He squeaked and twittered, and Harrod gestured with his reptilian head.

"You want me to climb back on?" I asked dubiously.

He nodded at me and lowered his head back down so I could do so. I straddled his shoulders, holding the sword in case we needed it again. Though I didn't doubt Harrod could just eat anything we came against in his current state, being a dream world, I didn't take anything for granted.

Muscles bunched up beneath me and then exploded, launching us into the air. The cavern roof above us had disappeared, and as we flew higher, light returned. Natural light, like a warm summer day. Wind whipped at my eyes and my vision blurred. I blinked and looked down to see what lay below. We flew over a castle, or the ruins of one. As we circled a tower, it gave way at the base, crumbling and falling to the ground in a puff of dust. I held up an arm to shield my face from the tiny specks of rubble that rose in a cloud around us.

I looked to where Harrod was flying. In the centre of the crumbling castle rose a white column. The ivory tower. Opius would be in there. Though it was still whole, cracks ran up the walls and paint flaked off in big chunks. The damage around us must reflect the state of Opius's health.

Going by what we could see from this height, he didn't have long. He had to let us go, I'd exhausted my gift on Harrod and I had no idea how to use it to get us out of here. I wasn't sure how I'd make

Opius release us from his dream. Hope, pure, blind hope was all I had left.

Harrod circled around the tower. There were no windows or doors that we could see. Before I'd figured out a way to get in, Harrod landed on the peaked roof. Then, he ripped it off.

That's one way to do it. I climbed off Harrod's back, balancing precariously on the edge of a wall. He used his tail to assist me down into the room. As I stepped in, the room righted itself, debris flying towards the ceiling to repair the damage. A muffled roar from outside and the sound of claws scrabbling at the roof.

"I let *you* in because I need something from you. The beast stays outside."

I turned to find Opius sitting in a chair facing me. My heart stopped, then restarted at twice its usual speed.

"You're dying, Opius," I said. "There's nothing you can do to stop it."

"I know."

"Then what could you possibly want from me?"

Opius stood and ran his eyes over me. As he did, I felt the worst of my injuries heal. Not completely, but enough. He walked to a window that materialised as he approached. It looked out over London. I watched him, unsure of how I felt. Part of me was angry, hated him, but after everything I'd seen of his past, I also felt sad. Not at his death, but at what had been taken from him in life. I felt sad for who Opius could have been, not the man he'd turned into—a bitter, selfish old man.

"I can free you. I can let you go."

"I can free myself." I hoped that was true.

"But not him," he said, eyes looking towards the ceiling at where I assumed Harrod sat. He said the words as a statement of fact, with no hint of malice or regret.

He believed it, but I didn't know if he understood my gift enough to know for sure. I knew I could affect another person with my gift, but I'd tried to force Harrod out of the dream and only partially succeeded. Was I not strong enough, or did I just not know how to use it properly? The room shook and a crack appeared in the glass of the window. Opius himself stumbled, his legs giving out from underneath him. By reflex, I put a hand out to steady him but he caught himself on a walking cane that appeared out of nowhere.

Clearly embarrassed at his weakness, he turned his head away from me, back to the window. As a child he'd been taught all his life that weakness was a failure and here he was, unable to even keep his feet in front of a half-blood. In that moment, I felt sympathy for him. Not much, and not even close to forgiveness, but sympathy. He waved a hand and the chair slid over to him. As he sat, the cane vanished.

"I know I've done terrible things. There is no justification for the crimes I have committed. I was desperate. I wanted to live, at any cost, and to have back the legacy that should have been mine." The tower shifted again and this time, plaster started peeling from the walls. Years of wear and neglect transformed the room in the space of moments. Opius was losing his hold on the dream world.

"You killed people, Opius. No matter what your background, how much you suffered, you did not have that right."

Opius nodded slowly. "That is why I'm giving you a chance to get your friend out."

"To make up for the people you murdered, you're leveraging the life of another? For your own gain?"

"No." Opius sagged in his chair, face wrinkled with age. Flecks of dust and paint were drifting down from the ceiling and some had settled on his robes. "I can't release you. I don't have the strength left, but there might be one who does."

Fear settled in the pit of my stomach. If Opius couldn't control his gift enough to pull it back and if I couldn't find a way out, Harrod could die. I could die.

"Where is Jones?"

"Jones?"

Opius looked to the cracked, dusty window. A scene played out behind it, similar to the ones I'd passed earlier in the dream. This time, young Mikael flung himself at the tutor, yelling at him. The vision was blurred but I could make out some details. Mikael's rat had escaped and been caught nibbling at the tutor's food. The tutor held the rat in his fist, squeezing it tightly over Mikael's head while he yelled. Mikael was distraught, tears running down his face while he tried to reach his pet. He managed to reach the tutor's hand and touch the rat. As he did, there was a shift in the vision, like a folding. The scene I watched slowed and blurred further, except for one thing. The rat. Its image sharpened and it continued to squirm as everything else ground to a stop. It struggled free, then scampered out of the window pane and into the dream world, then ran off. I reached into my pocket. Instead of the rat, I found the chess piece with his face.

"This is Jones?"

"Yes. To this day, I do not know how—" Opius stopped speaking and gasped in a painful breath. As he did so, the world around me rumbled and shook. Larger bits of debris started to fall around me and a rock hit my shoulder, sending me sprawling to the floor as I tried to dodge it. This time, the shaking building didn't settle. The tremor continued as the roof crumbled. The figurine I held fell and rolled across the sloping floor, coming to rest against the far wall.

"Jones!" Opius cried out, crawling across to retrieve it.

I followed him, scrambling around a beam that had fallen between us.

"Use the knife. You must use it! Jones will guide you out." I pulled out the knife.

"What about Harrod?" I yelled over the screaming sound of the world tearing apart around us.

"I'm sorry, it's too late. You must do it, do it now or you'll be trapped here."

Opius beckoned me towards him with one hand, as the other offered the carving. As I reached for it, he lunged forwards. He pushed me down and kneed me in the side while he clambered over me to wrench the knife out of my hands.

A tearing sound ripped the air apart and a portion of the tower slid away, and a section of floor beside me disintegrated. A wall tumbled down, rocks pelting us both as we grappled for the knife. Something heavy landed on my leg, pinning me as Opius raised the knife. Thunder rolled outside and the room swayed. Opius fell to the side, then rolled on top of me, thrusting with the knife. I caught it before it struck, pushing his arm back.

A bestial screech sounded outside, followed by the crashing rumble of a wall collapsing. A shower of pebbles and dirt fell over my face. Opius was lifted into the air above me, claws around his body drawing a stream of blood. The knife slipped out of his hand, landing near me. I strained to reach it. He struggled free, Harrod just managing to catch the end of Opius's robe on a sharp talon. I lay trapped under the rubble, Opius dangling over me at roof height. Just as my fingers found purchase on the knife, Opius crashed into the stone floor and landed with a wet crack onto my outstretched arm.

I looked over. Opius lay face down on the floor, body twisted and broken as it had been when I'd thrown him out of the window. This time, however, something protruded from his side. The bronze knife tip wasn't bloodied. I watched, dazed, as it sucked the life out of its previous owner

Everything exploded.

I was falling through a void. Bits of rubble and debris dotted the black surroundings, tumbling through space. Wind whipped against my skin as I plummeted towards nothing. Heart in my throat, I choked off a scream. My body tried to tear itself apart, limbs screaming in pain. I twisted around and looked for Harrod. He was himself again, a limp figure a little below me, just out of reach. Angling my body like a skydiver, I edged closer to him. Grabbing a sleeve, I pulled him towards me. *Jones*. I couldn't see him. The tearing in my body was too much and spots floated in front of my eyes. I realised the darkness had deepened, eating away the rubble that fell around us. I couldn't see anything but myself and Harrod. Then, just as blackness closed in and I started to numb, a stinging pain in my finger tickled the last of my consciousness. *Jones*.

I let the darkness take me.

Chapter Twenty-Four

As if from a deep sleep, my consciousness crept back to me. I sat, slumped into a carved chair next to a sleeping Harrod. Fuzzily, I looked around to see I was back in the parlour room of the Guardians.

"I am very glad to see you made it." The white-haired Guardian from the Other stirred a cup of tea as she looked me over.

"What happened? Why am I here?" I wrapped my arms around my middle, shivering. The Guardian handed me the cup and I held it, warming my face over the gentle steam it released.

"This is but a small detour. We simply wanted to see our charge was safe."

"Am I still in the dream?"

"No, child. The creature freed you, though I know not why." She lifted a hand to her face and, perched atop it, was Jones. The tiny rat nuzzled the Guardian's cheek before she dropped her hand again and the rat disappeared. "He guided you both out but I have snatched you from that path, so that we may speak. You will both wake, safe and well. Now, I believe you have something of ours?" She showed no impatience but sat with her hands folded gently in her lap.

"The other one—the Guardian that looks like a human child.

She said you didn't want it, that it was given away freely." I steeled my nerves. "Why should I give it back?"

"Because it has served its purpose. It is no longer needed in the world of Men. What havoc could be wrought if another found it?"

Angry, I told her it should never have been 'found' in the first place.

She laughed, a tinkling sound that sent chills through my already cold body. "Such demands, from one so young."

"I want no part in your schemes, Fae. The other one of your kind said—"

All mirth fled from the Guardian. "There is no other. We are one. All the Guardians are one. It is this that holds our world together and if we are sundered, all that we know will come to an end." Her voice was frightening, filling the room like a bad feeling and piercing my bones. Her face softened and her voice became gentle. "It is important you know this, child, for when you cleave us apart, you must know the weight of what you do. Remember, child. Always remember."

Jones appeared on her shoulder, chirruped, and darted down her arm before settling in her lap. I thought about the knife and what it could do.

"Will you promise it will be safe from the hands of men?" Though I wasn't in the habit of making demands from someone who could squash me like an ant, I had to try. "It won't make its way into our world again?"

The Guardian gave a secretive smile. "I shall promise that it will never be touched again by a man. I promise that you will never again be threatened by its existence."

I sighed. She couldn't lie, but she could twist her words to make something seem true when it wasn't. I thought it through but was too tired to poke holes in her words.

"Fine." I held out the knife.

She took it and slipped it into some secret pocket of her dress. Then, she kissed my forehead and I sank back into sleep.

A finger prodded my cheek, then lifted an eyelid. I flinched, forcing my eyes open to see Barg leaning over me. His face was upside down.

"Lady? Oh, Lady! Oh, Lady, I am so happy you are alive! You... *are* alive, yes?"

I tried to move, then stopped and grimaced as pain flooded my body. My arm was pinned by a soft, heavy weight and beneath it, my fist was clenched and cramped.

"What happened?"

"Barg is not completely, entirely, considerably sure Lady. Barg came in to check when Lady did not return. If Lady was in trouble and Barg did not come?" The hobgoblin shuddered. "That would not be a very good thing for Barg. When I came, the Lord was... well... like that!"

He tilted his head sideways, trying to look at me the right way up. I pushed the fleshy lump off of me. It was Opius. I scrambled back in a frantic panic, away from the dead body. Something hard hit me in the back and I looked up to see a crumbling golem standing to attention. A whimper left me before I realised it was dead, smooth stone now worn away into pitted ruins.

"Harrod. I have to find Harrod!" I stood, then winced.

A quick check showed none of my injuries were too serious, though I was covered in bruises like I'd been in a rockslide. Orange light flooded through the window and shadows still stretched long across the room. I retrieved my wand from the floor, but I didn't trace a light yet.

First, I wanted to get the hell out of this City and back to Harrod. Despite what the Guardian had said, I wouldn't be convinced he was safe until I saw it with my own eyes. Then, home.

Barg helped me out of the mansion. We stumbled through the streets of the Inner City, less careful about being seen. I didn't think anyone would find Opius at least until morning but that didn't mean

I wouldn't be remembered when he was. I knew I should lay low but I was too tired to do much about it.

Luckily, the streets were clear. The attendants of the Gala were most likely tucked up in bed right now, safe from the cold streets and rough half-bloods. When we got to the gate, Barg used the last of his vanishing powder to get us through. He grumbled about it loudly enough that I worried the guards would hear, but they were nearing the end of a long shift and didn't pay any attention to the noise.

The walk back to Harrod's went slowly. I was torn between wanting to hurry, and not wanting to face what lay ahead. The Guardian hadn't been very specific with her words and my bruises showed at least some of the damage carried through to the waking world. By the time we got to his door, exhaustion numbed my body. My head pounded and the contents of my stomach threatened to evict themselves on the doorstep. All were typical symptoms of Talent-burn, the effect of using more power than you were capable of. I wouldn't be able to think straight for days, let alone trace even a minor spell.

I walked up to the imposing entrance to Harrod's house. Instead of knocking on the door, I just stared at it for a moment. Then, I slumped onto the stoop and wept.

It was Gibble who found me. Barg, alarmed at my tears, had gone straight to him, and he'd come out to find me. Without speaking, he collected me up in his big strong arms and just held me for a moment.

"Little man is awake, Lady." His deep voice vibrated through my body. "You did be doing a stupid thing, but humans are stupid things, yes?" He leaned closer and dropped his rumbling voice to a whisper. "Your stupid thing did save him, though."

I laughed then, through tears and sobs. At my insistence, he put me down. Gibble was too polite to comment when I leaned on him heavily as we walked inside. Harrod sat in the sitting room, face pale and eyes creased in pain, but awake. I walked over and he stood, slowly. I wrapped my arms around him and together, we laughed.

～

"You're ok?" I asked as I wiped tears from my eyes.

"Yes. Emma, thank you, thank you so much for coming back for me…"

"Don't be ridiculous. I wasn't about to leave you there!" I collapsed into a couch and gratefully took a cup of hot coffee and some painkillers from Cym. Martin winked at me from across the room and I mouthed a 'thank you' to him.

"You risked your life for me," Harrod said, seeming confused as to why someone would do that for him.

"You did the same for me," I pointed out. "Opius was never after you, but you still got involved."

"Where is he now?" Martin asked and I flinched.

Harrod reached across to touch my shoulder. "Whatever happened, whatever you did, he deserved it. He's a killer, Emma, anything you did to stop that was a good thing, do you understand? Do *not* feel sorry for that bastard."

Tears trickled down my cheeks.

"You don't remember any of it, do you?"

"Not a damn thing."

"He's dead," I said in a quiet voice.

Martin sighed with relief but Harrod looked at me, still worried.

"When I got back, he was unconscious. He had a golem with him. It attacked me, then Opius pulled me into the dream." Tears filled my eyes. "Harrod, he had you chained up in there and… I saw things, I saw his life and what happened. I think… He's a bastard all right, but there's a reason. I don't know what to think. He was dying anyway, maybe this was a better way for him to go."

I explained most of what had happened in the dream world—the parts of Mikael's childhood, the dragon, and the rat. My hand slipped back in my pocket when I mentioned Jones. Being in the dream world had given him a kind of sentience. I hoped he'd be safe with the Guardians.

"Emma," Martin said, a note of worry in his voice. "How exactly did he die?"

"I'm not sure what did it in the end. In the dream, I stabbed him. Everything disintegrated, I'm not even sure how we got out." I wondered exactly what a lifetime inside a dream had bestowed upon a simple rat. "I killed him with the knife in the dream and when Barg found me, I'd stabbed him with it here, too."

"Where's the knife?" Harrod asked.

"The Guardians have it. They promised it would be safe."

Harrod nodded, seeming to agree that was the best place for it. Martin, however, had a wistful look to him. I could tell what he was thinking.

"Emma, what if you used the knife? You could have his power for yourself. You could be the strongest half-blood that ever lived, even if you only got Opius' Talent. Imagine if you had that kind of power, along with your own gift. You'd be unstoppable."

"No." I didn't even have to think about it. "Martin, I know you think that having Talent is amazing and wonderful... and it is, for the most part. But I saw what that power did to Opius and the lengths he went to trying to keep it. I don't want that."

He nodded in understanding, which surprised me. I knew he both worshipped and envied his brother, knowing that by rights, he should have been born with the same power. He showed himself as a cocky, confident person but that *had* to affect him.

Finally, after all our stories were told and when Deirdre and Bee had left, Harrod asked if I wanted to stay the night. When I shook my head, Gibble stood.

"Gibble be most happy if Little-man would have Lady driven home. Gibble can be carrying Lady, but perhaps Lady not be liking that?"

I laughed and accepted Harrod's immediate offer of a car and driver. He wanted to come, but I insisted he get some rest, and that Martin stay with him.

Gibble was waiting at the front door when the car dropped me off and together we went inside. He helped me with the door and chided Lenny for jumping on me when I entered. Finally, long after the sun had first broken the horizon, I slept.

~

It was three weeks until I heard from Greyson. That had surprised me—I'd sent him a message as soon as I could to let him know the half-blood killer had been taken care of. He stopped by my shop during a quiet spell, doffing his hat and standing awkwardly by the door until I was free.

"I got your message. I'm sorry it took me so long to respond."

"It's fine," I said. "I know you're busy."

"Busier than normal, actually. After recent events, I've been promoted. I'm now the lead DCI on the Otherworld Crime Unit." He had a look of forced optimism on his face.

"Oh, damn." The words were out before I could stop them. Everyone knew that a 'promotion' to the O.C.U. was career suicide. "I mean… congratulations?"

"No, it's ok. I'm looking at it as an opportunity." He picked up a box of Virility tea, then blushed and put it down when he read the label. "This department needs to exist, now more than ever. I'm going to make it what it should be."

"Lofty goals. Do you think they'll let that happen?"

"They won't have a choice. The press would have a field day if they were seen to be blocking any genuine effort to improve the department. I think I can do this, but I'll need help." He looked at me, expectantly.

"Anything I can do, just let me know."

He nodded as if he'd known what my answer would be. My answer was genuine. I would help, and I knew Harrod and Martin would too. Deirdre wouldn't hesitate and there were probably others in the City who would do what was needed.

He turned to go, then hesitated with his hand on the door. He coughed, straightened, then turned back to me.

"I don't suppose you'd be free for dinner tomorrow night?"

"Sure I... Oh, you mean a date?"

He nodded, a mortified look on his face.

"Tomorrow. After six, so I have time to close up shop and get ready."

He barked a laugh and left with a grin on his face, as I wondered what had come over me. I hadn't gone on a date in *years*.

Later that evening, I contemplated everything that had happened over the last few weeks. The mortal media had somehow found out Opius was behind the killings, and that a half-blood had been the one to stop him. Thankfully, my name hadn't been leaked, though I'd had reporters coming by to ask for comments on 'the situation'. This had led to the Talented releasing news of the new council appointments early, which had caused an uproar in itself.

Though people protested in solidarity with the 'unknown half-blood vigilante', others wanted all Talents gone from mortal society completely, bringing back the period of segregation. There was even a petition for the Fae to intervene—no chance of *that* happening, unless they had a scheme of their own afoot.

For me, it all made little difference, except for losing some customers and gaining others. My shop was busier, though I now had a few gawkers about; that had never been an issue before. The fights between Other-folk had stopped, thanks to Gibble who was now back to his normal self. I'd gained a regular dog walker, in the form of a hobgoblin who worked in exchange for 'fluffy flower juice'. Lenny was finally picking up, and back to his old self except for a more voracious appetite and a penchant for green apples. Olfred had been to check on him twice. On the second visit, he'd introduced me to his new assistant—a white rat. I blinked when I saw it and it stared back at me. Could it be Jones? There was no way to find out.

A short while later, Harrod and Martin walked in. They didn't wait for me—Martin took a seat in the corner while Harrod popped into my kitchenette to make tea for the three of us. When he was done, I joined them, leaving Gibble to take care of the shop.

"I spoke to Greyson. He's going to try and whip the O.C.U. into shape."

"Demotion, huh?" Martin said.

"He's going to make the best of it. He said he wants to make it what it should be, instead of the lip service it currently is."

"I'm sure he'll do well with it," Harrod said without looking up from his tea. "Oh, I have something for you—a friend of mine was close enough to overhear Opius's conversation with Aveline. They were talking about ways to discourage swamp gnats crossing over from the Other and bothering thoroughbreds. My friend breeds them, so he was eavesdropping the whole time. They never mentioned you."

It was no guarantee that Ave wouldn't hand me over to a killer at a moment's notice, but I did feel a little better hearing that.

"Now," Harrod said. I winced at his tone, knowing what he was about to say. "We really need to talk about these invitations. You know the Talent Lords are dying to meet you properly, half the City wants to throw a gala or host dinner just to have you there. Bee's already insisting on dressing you for all of them, free of charge. She *never* works free of charge."

I shook my head at him, smiling as his chatter washed over me. He'd been trying to convince me to enter society in an official capacity, hoping it would help with the efforts towards equality. At first, I'd refused. After what had happened, I'd wanted nothing to do with a class of people that would allow my people to be killed by one of their own. Abnett had been by, though, offering me an official pardon for killing Opius. Abnett had known my father and after we talked, I had headed out to Father's grave.

Dad would have wanted me to do this. He had fought for it, possibly given his life for it, and though I hadn't known he was doing it at the time, there was no doubt it was, in part, because of me. As I stood there in the warm sun, feeling the breeze on my cheeks, a deep longing struck me. Not just to see him again... to do him proud. To continue his legacy. To win his fight.

I sat back in my chair. Harrod had taken my lack of an answer as agreement and was already listing who to see and when, while Martin offered to take me to as many dress fittings as I needed. I laughed at that, knowing the reason behind it – he was terrible at hiding the lovestruck sparkle in his eyes whenever he spoke of Bee.

Gibble came over with a tray of biscuits and the rest of the afternoon was spent with good friends and a feeling of hope that maybe, one person could change things after all.

Also by Amy Hopkins

Love the book?

Check out these series from the author:

~

A New Dawn

Penny and Boots

The Adventures of Henry Mack (coming 2022)

~

You can sign up for updates and offers at:

www.amyhopkinsauthor.com

www.facebook.com/thespellscribe

www.twitter.com/spellscribe